God, how did she ever get into this mess?

"You two have been charged with possession of illegal weapons."

Vivian relaxed slightly. If they'd matched her prints, the kidnapping charges would've come up.

"Before we start, would you like anything to drink?"

"Can we just get this over with?" She realized that she was biting her lower lip and stopped.

"I'm not sure that Russell Cotters would like that."

"Who?"

"Deputy Cotters." He walked back and sat across from her. "You know, the officer that we found strangled to death in your hospital bathroom this morning."

God no. They had her.

"I don't know what you're talking about," she said.

"Drop the act, Vivian. We know you're not Sarah Hoffman. You're only going to dig yourself deeper."

"He was dead when I woke up," she said.

"Then how did you get out of the cuffs?" He paused, but what could she tell him? That a psychopath named Stromsky who worked for the Carmichael family had murdered that officer? What about the boys that Jarod had killed last night? They were going to pin this on her.

All of it.

She had nowhere left to hide…

Vivian Carmichael has been hiding in the San Bernardino Mountains for more than a year. Far from cell towers and video cameras, she thinks she's finally found a safe place to raise her four-year old son Cody. Until the night he crawls into her bed and whispers two words that fill her with terror.

"Daddy's home."

Now running for her life, she's horrified to learn that her estranged husband Jarod is not quite human anymore. Can she unravel the mystery of her family's dark secret before he can steal her son, claiming her as his next victim?

KUDOS FOR THE PORTAL

From the first page of *The Portal*, Christopher Allan Poe sets the scene for a chilling paranormal thriller that builds with cunning intensity in every chapter. Just when you think it's safe to take a breath...*wham*...the stakes are raised even higher, and now you're snared in the trap of a great book. You simply can't walk away... Evil lurks in many forms, and this is a strongpoint of Christopher Allan Poe's skill as a writer. *The Portal*'s villains aren't cliché. In fact, Jarrod can, in small ways, earn your sympathy as he relives moments from his fragmented childhood—little snapshots that have lead towards the corruption of his soul. –*Taylor, Reviewer*

The Portal is one of the best paranormal thrillers I've read in quite a while. Once I picked it up, I absolutely couldn't put it down. I just had to know what happened next. Poe painted a picture of a villain and a world that intrigued and fascinated even as it terrified me. Every time I thought the heroine was going to escape, something came along to trip her up. I think I'd bitten all my fingernails off by the end of chapter four.The world building and character development are superb, the story well written. One thing I especially liked was the number and variety of villains. Jarrod Carmichael, Kevin Stromsky, Mr. Vincent—I couldn't decide which one I hated most. They were all so perfectly despicable. And there is no shortage of good guys either. From four-year-old Cody and Vivian, his mother, to Detective Torres, the solid dependable cop, to Jay-Jay, a hoodlum with heart, the heroes battled for good against staggering odds...This one's a keeper, folks. – *Regan, Reviewer*

CHRISTOPHER ALLAN POE

THE PORTAL

A BLACK OPAL BOOKS PUBLICATION

GENRE: Paranormal Thriller

Published by Black Opal Books **http://www.blackopalbooks.com**

For Brandi,

Her knowing eyes,

And her loving smile.

I

THE LONG NIGHT

1

Vivian woke to an ocean of darkness that filled her lungs to capacity. Frantically, she groped her nightstand. Something banged on the floor. Where was her inhaler? There. She puffed and puffed again, but her short breaths could only take in so much.

Her chest loosened. Exhausted, she lay back. Underneath the splash of raindrops outside, Cody's muffled voice came from the hallway. Her bedroom door creaked open, and a sliver of light blinded her.

"Mommy?" His silhouette clung to the doorknob with one hand. The other dragged Mister Vincent on the floor behind him. "Are you okay?"

"Everything's fine." She lifted her blanket. "Come to bed."

Seconds later, he cuddled against her chest. She breathed deep the scent of baby shampoo. God she needed to be more careful. Just one slip and he would be alone in this world. Then what? Some chemical substitute to fill the void? Crime? Jesus, she would never let it come to that.

"Mommy," he whispered.

"Yes, sweetie."

"Mister Vincent is sorry."

She closed her eyes and prayed for sleep. Although Mister Vincent painted the kitchen walls in shades of peanut butter yesterday, whatever mess lay beyond her door could wait until morning. "It's fine."

"He didn't mean to let him in."

She almost sat up to check. No, everything was locked. The Trenton Security System was armed, and the dead bolts were three feet above the door handles. Well beyond Mister Vincent's reach.

"It was just a bad dream, baby," she said. "Not real."

He sat up on his knees and put his hands on her cheeks.

"Mommy," he said.

"Go to sleep."

"I have to tell you something, but I promised not to say it out loud."

"Fine," she said. "But then you'll lie down."

He nodded, leaned over her, and whispered in her ear, "Daddy's home."

She jumped up and turned on the light. It crashed to the floor. Her car keys! She needed them. They had to get out.

"Where is he? Where did you see Daddy?"

"Ouch," he cried.

She looked down and realized how hard she'd grabbed his shoulders.

"I'm sorry, baby," she said. "I didn't mean it." He lowered his head. "This is really important," she continued. "Like when Mommy needs her inhaler." He nodded. "I need you to tell the truth. Where did you see Daddy?"

"Walking in the trees."

She pulled up the mini blinds and wiped away the condensation on the window with her hand. Their van was parked next to the forest, at least thirty yards from the cabin. She put on her shoes and grabbed her keys.

"Come here," she said.

He ran in front of the toppled lamp. Shadows raced across the walls. She leaned down, and he wrapped his arms around her neck. In the hallway, her knees nearly buckled. The front door swung back and forth in the wind. Leaves blew through the living room into the hall.

Cody clutched his bear. "He didn't mean to let him in."

"I know he didn't, sweetheart. Don't worry. We'll make sure Mister Vincent stays safe." She hugged Cody's head against her shoulder. "We all need to be very quiet now."

Carefully, she stepped over the creaky second floorboard. Slowly. Don't panic. The power in the cabin went out. Shit. Following the meager light from the front door, she picked up her pace.

"I can't see." Cody's voice seemed to thunder.

"Shhh, you have to stay quiet."

The basement door directly behind her opened and clicked shut.

"Hello, Vivian." Jarod's voice froze her in place. His footsteps thumped close. Breath smothered the nape of her neck. "'Till death do us part. You do remember, don't you?"

She steadied her legs. Cody needed her to be strong.

"Honor and obey, too." Her joke, their joke failed to produce any laugh. He just kept breathing, heavy and slow in the darkness.

"I told you it was an accident," he mumbled, as if something filled his mouth.

"Cody almost died, you son of a bitch."

"You stole my fucking son," he shouted.

She bolted down the hallway. In her wake, his footsteps shook the cabin. She reached the front door, grabbed the handle, and slammed it shut behind her. A thud rocked the house. He must have smashed into it.

She almost continued, but stopped. He'd run three miles a day when they were married. Every single day. And she was carrying Cody. He could barrel them down within seconds.

She fumbled with her keys and locked the top bolt. Last month, she'd installed the dual key dead bolts to keep Cody from opening the door. Fat lot of good that did, but now they had a use far greater. There was no turn latch on the inside. Only a keyhole. And the bars on the windows meant that Jarod was now locked inside.

The door rattled. A thunk rumbled through the mountains. She took off for the car. Above, the storm clouds broke. Flashes of lightning exposed his Humvee parked off the driveway. They were more than an hour from any town. Visions of their capsized minivan, forced from the road by the military vehicle, filled her head.

Thwack. The repetitive cracking gave away Jarod's position as she raced to the Humvee. Inside the left wheel well, she found Jarod's magnetic Hide-A-Key. Thank god some things never changed. She unlocked the gigantic door and lifted Cody into the backseat.

"Put your seat belt on," she said.

"I'm sorry," he cried.

"Now."

She opened the driver's door and climbed into the vehicle. Switches and panel readouts sat all around her. Could she even drive this stupid thing? Where was the ignition? There. She turned the key. The engine roared.

"Mommy," Cody shouted.

Something snapped the glass. An explosion of nuggets sprayed her face. Jarod reached in and grabbed her sweater. She screamed. Broken and jagged, some fused together, his teeth dripped saliva.

The corners of his lips twisted as he shouted, "He's mine."

She punched the accelerator. Mud puddles sprayed over the windshield, blurring her view. Running alongside, Jarod yanked the steering wheel. The Humvee lunged toward a tree trunk and sideswiped it.

His shriek, guttural and inhuman, echoed through the cab. She slammed on the brakes to regain control. Something brushed her leg. His severed hand twitched in her lap. Forcing back her nausea, she slapped the thing onto the passenger floorboard and punched the gas.

At the end of the driveway, she turned left. Where could they go? Erika's house? No. If Jarod had found her here, he might have people waiting for her there.

For the last year, she'd planned for this, and none of it mattered. Along with their clothes and cash, she'd also left every inhaler behind as well.

In the backseat, Cody sobbed.

"It's okay, sweetie." She reached back to hold his hand but found only a toe. "It's over. We're safe now."

They could get out of this if she could just get down the mountain. Tammy probably still lived in Los Reyes. That was only a two-hour drive. They could *still* get out of this.

A blue dashboard light knocked back her hope as she sped around the final bend of Chesterfield Road. She closed her eyes and prayed over the sound of Cody's sobs. The gas gauge flashed empty.

2

Through the shattered window, mist, laced with the scent of pine, sprayed Vivian's face. Though the Humvee ate both lanes of traffic, and though speed would burn their fuel faster, she pressed the accelerator. The initial lead would count more.

"Where are we going?" The tremor in Cody's voice tore at her heart.

"Everything's fine now. We're going to see Aunt Tammy."

She checked her rear view mirror. So far nothing, but she couldn't shake Jarod's face from her mind. Something had deformed him. Those teeth. No, she must have seen it wrong. Some trick of the light or, more likely, her fear running wild.

In the backseat, Cody stared through the side window. He scrunched his hand on his knee repeatedly.

"Let's play a game," she said, not just for him. More than ever, she needed to hear his voice. "I spy the letter T."

"What?" He sounded distant.

"The letter T."

He finally turned from the window. "Tree."

"You always get me."

"I spy the letter M," he said quietly.

Although M was always Mister Vincent, she guessed, "Mouth." He shook his head. "Money?" She reached back and tickled his knee. "Where did you get money from? Did you rob a bank?"

In the rear view mirror, she saw him smile. At least on the surface, he seemed oblivious to Daddy's hand thumping the floorboard around every turn.

A blue and red glow filled the cab. A quick look back showed a police car's flashing lights.

"Damn," she said.

"Soap."

Jarod couldn't have called the police. The cabin didn't have a landline. And there weren't any neighbors for seven miles. Nor any cell towers until Mercer. Maybe the cop just needed to get around her. She slowed onto the shoulder of the road. His siren wailed.

"Shit," she said.

"Mommy."

"I promise I'll eat the whole bar when we get down the mountain. Now, I need you to be quiet."

To avoid Jarod coming up on them, she pulled onto a dirt road. Branches clawed and scratched at the tank-like vehicle. Gravel popped underneath the tires. They reached a circular clearing with metal fire pits surrounding the perimeter, no campers. She stopped and took a deep breath. If this officer ran her license, they'd add grand-theft-auto to her kidnapping charges.

She pulled down the visor and freaked. Her hair wisped every direction. Blood spattered her clothing. Quickly, she wiped her face and tied her hair in a knot. On the massive center console, she found his sport jacket. Jarod's musky cologne made her skin crawl as she put it on.

A spotlight drenched the cab of the Humvee, followed by approaching footsteps.

"License, registration, and proof of insurance." The officer's cold tone made her uneasy. She held up her hand to block his flashlight and realized just how far from civilization they were.

"What's the problem?" she asked.

"Do you know how fast you were going?"

"Maybe forty," she said.

They'd only driven fifteen miles. Too far to catch on foot, even for Jarod. But what if he could hotwire the minivan? She should've slashed its tires.

The officer lowered his light. This wasn't good. His crew cut and chiseled features looked like he came from a long line of ball busters.

"License and proof of insurance," he repeated firmly.

"It's around here somewhere." That sounded dumb. How many times had he heard those words? She opened the glove compartment and panicked. "I'm sorry."

Carefully, she pushed a gun back. "I must have left my purse at home."

Jarod. That bastard had brought a gun to the house where Cody slept.

"Have you had anything to drink tonight?" the officer asked.

"Excuse me?" She caught herself. With Cody in the car, she refused to drive under the influence of mouthwash. Still, losing her temper wasn't going to help. "No. Nothing to drink."

"Please step out of the vehicle."

If she did, he would see her splattered like a slasher victim. Then he'd find the hand.

"Whatever I did, can you please let me off with a warning? Just this once."

"The side of your vehicle looks like it was buffed with a chainsaw. Broken glass is everywhere. You have no license, registration, or side mirror for that matter. And your son is in the car with you."

"So is that a no?" She immediately regretted her tone, but the police always brought out the worst in her.

The jerk didn't respond. He just stared at her.

"If you smell my breath," she said. "Will you be able to tell that I'm sober?"

"A field sobriety test encompasses more than alcohol. Now get out, or I will remove you."

"My driving was bad because we're almost out of gas and I was trying to coast. And I didn't want to mention it, but the reason we're heading to town at his hour is for Midol. I'm having cramps."

His eyes became twitchy. He shifted from foot to foot. Men. Lies poured from their mouths without the slightest remorse. They could rape the earth and butcher children, but tell them it was that time of the month, and they fidgeted worse than Billy Graham at an orgy.

"What about your other gas tank?" he asked. She could feel his relief at the change of subject. Good. She had him on the ropes.

Wait...

"What did you say?" she asked. "Other gas tank?"

"This isn't your car?"

"It's my father's."

"Unlike other *civilian* models." His voice carried an air of disdain. "The Humvee comes standard equipped for all combat situations. Hit that switch on the left."

She searched the dashboard and flipped the button. The gas gauge slowly filled.

"God, I could kiss you," she said.

"That's nice of you, but I still need you to step out of the vehicle."

There weren't any more excuses. He would take her to the station. Her fingerprints would show that she was wanted, and Jarod would make sure they locked her away forever. A lifetime without Cody. Forcing back her tears, she knew what had to be done.

"I just remembered where the registration is." She reached into the glove compartment, grabbed the gun, and pointed it at his head. He jumped back and went for his weapon.

"Don't even think it."

"Mommy." Cody sounded concerned.

"We're just playing cops and robbers," she said without turning back. Then she opened the car door. "Cuff yourself to that campfire grate."

"Don't do anything you're going to regret," the officer said.

"Any minute now." She hushed her voice. "My ex-husband will come down that mountain. He is going to steal my son and kill me. Don't think for one second that I won't shoot you if I have to."

"Whatever the problem is, we can work it out."

Though he held one hand forward, the other rested on his holstered firearm. She knew he was working up the guts to call her bluff.

"Put that gun on the ground and kick it to me," she said. "Or I will shoot you in your stomach twice and then sleep like a baby tonight." She shoved the gun toward him and shouted, "Now."

"Okay." He held both hands forward.

When the gun was at her feet, she said, "Now chain yourself to the grate."

"If your husband is really after you like you say." He cinched the cuff around his wrist. "It's smarter to let us help."

"Like you helped us before? Thanks for the concern, but he owns you."

"I don't even know your damn husband."

"Maybe not you, but certainly the people above you," she said. "Just cuff yourself."

"You're making a mistake."

Once she was positive he was restrained, she opened the car door and got inside. Through the missing window, she said, "When we reach the bottom of the mountain, we'll call somebody to pick you up."

Vivian sped off, terrified of this new world she inhabited—where the two guns in her lap made her feel safer than none at all.

At the main road, she stopped. What was that? Even over the rumble of the engine, she heard a clicking noise from the back. Great. Now, the car was breaking down. What else could go wrong tonight?

Again, click click. That wasn't the car. Click. It was coming from inside the cab. Right behind Cody.

Jarod couldn't have made it this far. Or could he? In the confusion with that cop, she hadn't been able to watch the vehicle the entire time. She opened the door and got out. Then she crouched low and crept to the back bumper. With her gun ready, she pulled open the rear hatch.

It was empty. No, there was that noise again. A chill raced up her spine as she saw it. Jarod's hand. Mangled tendons and shattered bone. Inch-long hooked talons extended from where the fingernails should have been. But even that couldn't compare with that horrible click of bony claws against the wheel well as the hand twitched.

The thing was still moving.

3

Vivian parked at the back of the K Street cul-de-sac, just past Tammy's trailer. Above, the only working streetlamp flickered and throbbed. Three houses down, a group of black-booted peckerwoods hovered around a truck on blocks. Spray paint cans hissed from their direction.

Perfect. Five minutes, and already her lungs felt tight, strangled in barbed wire and oil-soaked dirt. She had promised herself that night to never come back, and now she'd brought Cody here.

Still, none of that mattered. They had bigger problems. What had happened to Jarod? His face? She tried to push the image away, but those claws. He'd been dangerous before. Now he wasn't even human.

Worse yet, if he could find them at the cabin, no place would be safe. Especially Erika's house. They needed to leave the country. That meant retrieving the cash she'd stashed. No way she could attempt it with Cody in tow. So suck it up, Vivian. Even at three AM without a courtesy phone call, big sis was her best option.

"It's okay," she whispered to Cody, who stirred as she pulled him from the backseat. He didn't wake. Then she grabbed the ice chest from the front seat.

All right, maybe storing Jarod's disgusting, twitching claw in a beer cooler wasn't too safe. She packed it tight with towels though, and the chest *was* wrapped in duct tape, too. That counted for something. Besides, it was proof that she wasn't crazy. Maybe, it could be her chance to come out of hiding. Sole custody even. She didn't dare think it. Hope was a useless emotion, reserved for gamblers throwing away their money. She didn't have that luxury. In any case, the claw wouldn't leave her sight.

Tammy's gate almost fell from its hinge as Vivian opened it. She walked to the front door and knocked. Just feet away, the neighbor's pit bull chomped and rattled a chain link fence. She rang the bell. *Please let this be the right decision.* Through the rusted screen, she saw the door open.

"Knock it off."

Vivian recognized her sister's voice.

"Sorry, I didn't mean to—"

"Not you." The porch light turned on and the screen creaked open. "The damn dog."

Vivian's knees weakened. That brick-colored hair pulled into a bun. Her piercing green eyes. For a second, she thought she was staring at her mother.

"You look like hell," Tammy said. She even sounded like their mother. Had this been a mistake?

"I'm sorry if we woke you," Vivian said.

"Well I don't sleep in my work clothes."

Looking down at the Astro Lounge insignia on Tammy's jacket, Vivian covered her embarrassment with a cough. Tammy couldn't have been one of the dancers. A bartender? Maybe, but judging from her bulk, she was more likely a bouncer.

"It's been awhile." Tammy motioned to Cody, who slept soundly. "Yours?"

She nodded. "This is Cody."

The skinheads behind them began shouting.

"Well," Tammy said. "You might as well come in before Anthony and his boys start humping your leg."

As she walked inside, the scent of beef and cigarettes tightened her chest even more. This wasn't asthma though. A polluted flood of memories made her nervous.

She laid Cody on a couch in the unlit living room and covered him with an afghan. In the kitchen, she found Tammy sitting at a Formica table. A hanging light swayed as she poured two shots of Wild Turkey.

"None for me," Vivian said.

"Who said anything about you?" She slammed one of the shots. The idea of leaving Cody here, even for just a few hours, seemed crazier by the minute. But with no money for food, gas, or a motel, they were out of options.

"What's in the chest?" Tammy asked.

"Food."

"And the duct tape is for what, freshness?"

"It wouldn't stay shut." She wished she had a chain and padlock for the thing.

Tammy eyed her. Then she took a drag from her cigarette. "Well, it better not be drugs. You know I won't expose my family to that."

"It's not." Vivian felt a little ashamed because two handguns and a severed claw were far worse than any narcotic on earth. "Did you say, family?"

Tammy motioned to a white cat walking across the stove. "That's Sinead." She scratched another tabby napping in a chair next to her. "I took in Bones after Mom died." She paused. "We missed you at the funeral."

"I know," she said. "I really wanted to go."

"So why didn't you?"

This conversation couldn't lead anywhere good. Every wasted moment only played in Jarod's favor, so she said, "Tammy, I need your help."

"You don't waste time."

"I'm sorry, but we're in trouble." Vivian sat down at the table. "I need to borrow your car and some money for gas."

"How did I know this was coming?"

"You know I hate to ask, but—"

"I'm your last hope."

God, she hated when Tammy did this. Taunted and teased. Dangled the prize just out of her reach.

"If you could watch Cody," she said. "I'll back in two hours, tops."

"Let me guess, the mob is after you."

"Tammy, please. This is serious."

"The secret police?" Her laugh echoed in the kitchen. Furious, Vivian didn't dare speak. Tammy put out her cigarette in the tray. "I'll tell you what's going to happen. You're going to disappear and dump your brat on me."

Vivian stood up so fast, that her chair nearly knocked over. "Don't ever speak about my son like that."

"Fair enough, as long as you tell me why."

"What?" Vivian asked.

"After all this time. You show up at my doorstep, begging."

"Begging?" She couldn't believe what she was hearing. "How many times have I bailed you out?"

"What? Ten years ago? You must be joking."

"I just need you to watch Cody for a few hours. I can even pay you when I'm done."

"Oh this is good." Tammy poured herself a new shot. "Tell you what. I'll do it if you give me the real reason you're here. Why me?"

"Because—"

"Why now? And don't give me this sisterhood bullshit."

"Because I never told Jarod about you," she snapped. "He doesn't know where to find us here."

The sarcastic smile left Tammy's face. Silence filled the kitchen. The kind that only their mother had been able to create.

"Tammy, listen."

"No, it makes sense. You always were ashamed of us."
She began petting Bones. "Thought you were so much
better. And maybe you were. You got his looks and her
brains."

"I don't know why I didn't tell him."

"I get it," Tammy said. "But what I can't figure is with
all of that." She waved her hands as if demonstrating a door
prize. "Why you couldn't resist stealing Mom's boyfriend."

"Excuse me?"

"Kenny wasn't much, but he was all she had."

"Exactly what do you think you walked in on?"

"Jesus, Vivianna, I'm not a fool."

There it was. The name her mother had called her.
Suddenly her anger felt like a swarm of hornets in her
stomach.

"I want to know what you think you saw," Vivian said.

"Let's just drop it."

Oh, it was far too late. "You want to know why I
didn't come to the funeral. Why I ran away and never told
the man I married who I really was?"

"Sorry I brought it up," Tammy said.

"That drunk piece of shit Kenny tried to rape me. And
you know what our mother said to me? She told me not to
ruin it for her. That I had already ruined everything else."

"Didn't you?"

"Are you insane? I was sixteen." The tears in her eyes
didn't ease her rage. They magnified it. "That's why I ran
away. And I didn't go to her funeral because I was afraid.
Terrified that the only reason I cried was because I would

never get the chance to tell that bitch what I really thought of her."

Tammy just sat with a stupid sneer, rubbing her finger across the rim of her shot glass.

Something brushed Vivian's hand. She glanced down to find Cody. He didn't speak. Instead, he leaned his head against her leg, with a look of concern that quieted her anger instantly. Again, silence filled the trailer.

Finally, she wiped her eyes. "I've spent too many years blaming myself." She picked up Cody in one arm and grabbed the cooler. "I don't know what the hell I was thinking. I wouldn't leave my son with a cockroach like you for a second."

She hurried back to the front door.

"Don't ever come back here again you—"

Vivian slammed the door and cut her off. She breathed deep the smoggy air. Somehow, she felt better. Maybe it had been bottled up for too long. Or maybe, the curse of genetics had provided her with one final opportunity to tell her mother off. Either way, she did feel better. Cleansed.

She was crossing the street when she heard the voices. Three skinheads surrounded the Humvee.

"Well," the short one with beady eyes said. "Look who's back."

She held Cody tight. After the night she'd had, these bastards had no clue of what they were getting themselves into.

⁙

As Vivian left, Tammy thought of a million things that she should've said. At least the slut was gone. Good riddance. Take her lies with her. She poured another shot and slammed it down. Wild Turkey usually calmed her nerves after work, but not tonight.

He doesn't know where to find us here, Vivian had said. There could only be one reason why she came here when she was in trouble and not the police station. Only one reason.

"I'll show you a fucking cockroach." She picked up the phone and dialed nine-one-one.

4

Vivian stared at the three skinheads, lined in a row between her and the car. Above, the streetlamp seemed close to giving out altogether. Even in this dim light, she saw that the boys couldn't have been older than eighteen. The worst age. Too young and dumb to know they had nothing to prove.

What could she do? In one arm, she held Cody. In the other, she carried the cooler. Stay calm. Predators tended to attack when they sensed fear. Jarod always did.

She glanced back at Tammy's house just as the porch light shut off. Whatever bridge existed between them had just been destroyed. The guns? No, they were taped inside the cooler to keep them from Cody. She wouldn't be able to get to them before these guys grabbed her.

"Please step aside." She tried to sound confident.

"Does that hurt?" Cody asked. He might have been talking to the tall guy on the right. More than a half dozen metal piercings sprouted from his lips and eyebrows. Or maybe he was asking the short one in the middle. Tattoos stained the left side of his neck.

"Be quiet, baby," she said. Then she turned back to the boys. "Move away from my car now."

"Anything you say." Tattoo man stepped to the side, exposing a giant black X spray-painted on the side of the tan Humvee. Great. As if the damaged, stolen car wasn't noticeable enough. Now a bull's-eye was painted on the side, too.

"Did you take art classes for that?" she asked.

Noticing the smell of stale rubber, she looked down and found a knife sticking from her flat front tire.

"Looks like somebody messed up your ride." Tattoo man reached over and pulled the blade. Then he caressed it between his thumb and forefinger.

"I don't have any money." She stepped back.

"Quit it," his pierced companion said. "She's got a kid with her. You're scaring them."

"They should be frightened," Tattoo Man said.

"Well you're scaring me, too. I just got out of lockup."

"Will you shut the fuck up, Phil?" He pointed the knife at his friend. "You sound like my mother."

"Dude, don't fucking use my name in front of her."

"I'll do anything I want," he said. "How is anyone supposed to fear the Edge if you wet your pants every five seconds?"

"Okay Anthony Jessup, graduate of Lincoln Memorial," Phil said. "Let's spread the word."

As she watched them argue, the words 'Minor Threat' on Tattoo Anthony's shirt seemed to apply more and more. Her fear earlier seemed premature, even foolish. "Look guys, I really don't have any money."

"You think we want your oil money?" Anthony asked.

"I don't know what you want. Maybe you're mad because you lost World War II."

That got all of their attention. Their baby-faced companion stepped forward and broke his silence. "Just because we're skins doesn't make us Nazis lady."

"People are so dumb." Phil seemed genuinely hurt.

"Are you kidding me?" she asked. One day, she and Cody might laugh until they cried about this night. As it stood right now, she just wanted to strangle these kids. "My sister is right through that door. Now help me change the tire before I call the cops."

"Tammy's your sister?" Baby-face asked.

How should she answer that question? Knowing Tammy, she probably treated these idiots like her cat family. Finally she nodded.

"Vivian?" he asked.

"How do you know my name?"

"I'm Jason Daniel."

That sounded familiar, but she couldn't place him.

"Jay-Jay," Cody whispered in her ear.

She almost told him to be quiet but stopped. He was right. A weird feeling settled in her stomach. It couldn't be Jay-Jay. Where were his towhead curls? This couldn't be the boy that cried raindrops because she wouldn't let him stay up to watch *Home Alone 3*.

"Jay-Jay?" she asked.

He nodded. Chills rose on her neck because Cody hadn't even been born when she knew Jay-Jay. Somehow Cody knew his name.

"Knock it off." Jay-Jay turned to Tattoo Anthony. "She's cool."

Anthony shook his head. "She's destroying the earth for all of us."

"Of course," she said. After the night that she'd had, it made sense. "Skin head eco-terrorists."

"No." Anthony huffed.

"We're straight edge," Phil chimed in.

"Whatever you say." Though she felt quite safe now, she couldn't help wonder if she was witnessing the birth of something more sinister. Had Timothy McVeigh once cut his terror teeth on single mothers at four in the morning?

"Straight edge is our life. We don't need no strife." Jay-Jay must have been reciting lyrics, because his words carried the slightest melody. Clearly punk music. "Straight edge for every boy and girl, before these fools destroy the world."

"How deep," she said, and Jay-Jay nodded.

Anthony closed the switchblade and put it in his pocket. "You've had your chance and all you do is pollute your bodies until you can't think straight. Then you pollute the world with this thing."

"One, I don't even drink alcohol. And two, it's not my car," she said. "Now, my son's in pajamas and it's freezing. Either help me change the tire, or get out of my way."

Cody giggled, clearly enthralled that somebody besides him was being ordered around.

"Why should we help you?" Anthony asked.

Arguing with a teenager could take all night, and Jarod was searching for them now.

"Because in here." She held the cooler forward. "I have important documents to bring to the media. The government will stop at nothing to silence me."

"No shit?" Jay-Jay and Phil asked at the same time. Anthony still eyed her.

"The Exxon Corporation has been channeling funds to terrorist groups in Somalia," she said. "The documents in this cooler can cripple them, but I need my tire changed so I can get to CNN."

"That's exactly what I'm talking about." Anthony looked at his friends. Then he punched Phil in the shoulder. "Well don't just stand there. Help the woman."

"You're the one who slashed her tire."

"I don't care who's responsible," Vivian said. "We need to hurry."

The squeal of brakes a few blocks down seemed to accentuate her lie. She looked up to find a dark sedan speeding toward them. Jarod couldn't have found her so fast.

A thundering rhythm grew rapidly in volume. From above, a spotlight beam lit the entire street. A helicopter hovered. Anthony darted for a chain-link fence.

"Follow us." Jay-Jay grabbed the cooler before she could stop him. He chucked the ice chest over the fence and squeezed through a padlocked gate. Behind them, the sedan screeched to a halt. Both she and Cody fit through the gap in the chain with ease.

Waste-high weeds and soft dirt slowed her down as she raced through the field. Glancing back, she saw two of Jarod's thick-chest thugs struggle with the gate. Intense wind scattered the weeds in all directions. Somebody grabbed her. She spun to find Jay-Jay pointing to the canal in front of them.

"There's an entrance to the storm drain up ahead," he shouted. She clutched Cody and followed him. From behind her, the spotlight seemed to shine brighter now. The helicopter must've landed in that field.

Jay-Jay held her free hand. They moved down a steep concrete embankment. At the bottom, she slipped and dropped to one knee. The chilly stream splashed up to her waste, but she managed to hold Cody above the water line. She got to her feet and followed Jay-Jay down the wash. Then underneath the roadway.

Above, speeding cars vibrated the overpass. In the drainage culvert, Jay-Jay pulled open a vertical storm grate that led to a dark tunnel.

"It's okay, baby. It's just going to be a little cold." She pushed Cody underneath. Next she slipped into the tunnel. The grate clanged shut.

"Keep going straight," Jay-Jay said through the metal rebar. "It will be really dark. Just keep your hands on the right wall, and you'll end up at a steel ladder. It will take you to the junkyard."

"She's not up here," somebody shouted in the distance.

"Anthony and Phil are probably already there," Jay-Jay whispered.

"Wait," she said. "What about you?"

"I know a hundred short cuts. Take my light." He handed his keys through the grate and then held up the water cooler with Jarod's hand in it. "I'll bring the documents to the junkyard. Meet you there." He backed away. Ridiculously loud, he shouted, "You bastards think you can stop the Edge?"

He tore off down the wash. Maybe thirty seconds later, a chorus of splashing footsteps raced by.

"There," a deep voice shouted. Then, only the babble of rushing water.

With Cody in one arm and the light in the other, she turned to face the tunnel. Guck squished in her shoes. The blue key light showed little more than foam and street debris on the water's surface, which reached just below her knees. Darkness sprawled beyond.

"Don't worry, Mommy," Cody whispered in her ear. "It will be okay."

"I know," she said, unable to imagine how things could get worse. She had no inhaler, food, money, or vehicle now. And all of their hopes to elude Jarod's people rested on an eighteen-year-old punker.

6

Despite her efforts, Vivian couldn't avoid the water that splattered all around. In brooding shades of dark blue, the tunnel looked like a cavern, filled with eyes that stalked the darkness, just beyond the light's reach.

"Stop it." She sloshed forward. When Cody didn't listen, she grabbed his hand and pulled it away from the rainwater streams that dumped into the tunnel every few feet. Since he wouldn't understand the danger of radiator fluid and other toxic chemicals, she said, "People pee on the street up there."

His hand shot back around her neck. "Gross."

"Very gross." She tried not to think about the fact that every inch of her clothing clung to her body.

A splash came from the tunnel opening to their left. She spun and shined the light to find a dam of twigs and debris. A rotting stench wafted from that area, so she turned back and picked up her pace. The drainage pipe finally ended at a concrete wall, embedded with ladder rungs.

"Thank God," she said.

Above, storm runoff dripped from the perimeter of an open manhole cover. Was it a trap? Jarod's people could be waiting up there. No, Anthony and Phil had probably left it open, but she couldn't take the chance.

"I need to make sure it's safe above." Although she hated the idea, she set Cody down in the stagnant water that came to his waist. "Stand by the ladder so I can see you."

She gave him the keys and showed him the button. "Push this for the light." The minute she took her finger away, the darkness seemed to swallow them. A loud splash, this time at their feet.

"Cody, what was that?" His arm pulled from her grip. She shouted for him and reached out, but caught only air.

"Mommy," he cried. Finally the light flicked on. She looked down. He clutched the button with both thumbs. Mister Vincent floated face-up at their feet with his left eye hanging out.

She dropped to one knee and held Cody tight. In the confusion, she hadn't noticed him carrying the teddy bear this entire time, but she should have. They'd been inseparable, ever since she'd run from Jarod.

"Don't leave," he said. Her heart broke when she saw his tears. How could she be so stupid?

"I'm sorry, baby. I wasn't thinking." She wiped his cheeks and kissed his forehead. "You know that I would never leave you, right?" He nodded. "We'll go up together. I'll carry Mister Vincent."

He gave her a strange look as she picked up the bear from the water. They climbed the ladder with Cody on the inside. At the top, she pushed him through and then picked him up. Though nothing could really protect him from the downpour, she smothered him with both arms and ran.

Dead ahead, two high-powered floodlights sat at the top of a pole, illuminating the rain. Hundreds of crippled cars lay all around. Some stripped. Others were stacked into piles that seemed on the verge of tipping. She followed the lights to a metal warehouse, large enough to house a seven forty-seven.

"I'm cold," Cody said.

"I know, but look at that." She pointed to an enormous magnet crane and ran up to the warehouse. Peeking inside the door, she found Anthony and Phil sitting next to a trashcan fire. Even without Jay-Jay, she had to take her chances with them. The steel door shrieked as she slid it open.

"What are you doing here?" Anthony jumped up.

"Jay-Jay invited us. We're going to warm up."

"Bullshit," he said. "You're going to bring those assholes back here."

"Nobody followed us." She was pretty sure it was true. "Now move aside. My son is freezing."

When she tried to walk around him, he stepped between her and the fire.

"You can't stay," he said.

"Listen jerk, we just spent the last ten minutes in a storm drain because of you."

"Assholes," Cody added.

"That's right, baby, this is an asshole. Now either move out of my way, or I place an anonymous call to the cops and tell them that you're squatting in this garage at night."

"Dude." Phil punched Anthony's chest. "Why do you always have to be such a jerk?"

"We'll leave soon enough." She shouldered her way past them and sat in front of the fire.

Her body and face warmed instantly. Flames licked just below the mouth of the trashcan. Luckily, the warehouse stood at least three stories, giving the smoke plenty of room to drift. Phil and Anthony returned.

She removed Cody's pajamas, leaving him in his Hulk underwear.

"Don't you think it's ironic that your base is a garage?" She rung out Cody's shirt.

"What?" Phil studied the collection of stripped vehicles, grease puddles, and engine blocks on the concrete floor. Anthony pouted with his back to them.

"Well aren't you guys environmentalists?" she asked.

"It's the only place that stays unlocked at night."

Black smoke poured off of the trash can fire as well. Not to mention the spray paint cans they used to tag the

Humvee, but she decided against saying anything. She needed the heat more than she needed to make them feel stupid.

"Where are your documents?" Phil asked.

"What do you mean?"

"You know," he said. "The ones to bring down Exxon."

She'd forgotten all about her story.

"Jay-Jay has it," Cody answered for her, letting her know once again that he understood far more than he let on.

A hollow feeling settled in her stomach. Mother's intuition. Maybe it was nothing at all, but suddenly the strange things that had happened tonight didn't seem so coincidental.

"Give me a minute." She turned away from Phil, grabbed Cody's pajamas, and began dressing him. "I need to ask you a question, baby."

He nodded but didn't look up at her.

"How did you know Jay-Jay's name earlier?" she asked. He poked her chest, so she said, "No games right now. This is important. Mommy needs to know who told you Jay-Jay's name."

"Mister Vincent."

"Cody, tell the truth."

"He told me."

Clearly this wasn't going to work. She picked up the soggy bear with its creepy hanging eye. "Mister Vincent has no mouth. See, it's all sewn up. How could he tell you?"

"That's not Mister Vincent."

For a second, she wanted to throw it in the fire. Had she picked up somebody else's bacteria-infested bear from the storm drain? Then she saw the bleach spot on its ear from last Christmas. "Cody, stop lying."

"I'm not." He looked at her like she was crazy. "That's not Mister Vincent."

"Then who is this?"

"That's my bear."

If Mister Vincent wasn't his bear, whom had he been talking about for the last year? An actual person? No. She'd been carrying Cody when he'd told her Jay-Jay's name. Nobody else was around. Ice raced through her veins. Cody's words at the cabin. *Mister Vincent is sorry. He didn't mean to let him in.*

"If this isn't Mister Vincent, then where is he now?" she asked. He looked around the garage. When he didn't answer, she held his chin gently and caught eye contact. "Where is he?"

"He'll come back."

The front door screeched, and Vivian jumped. Jay-Jay ran inside.

"About time," Phil said. "I thought they caught you."

Jay-Jay didn't speak. He just stood by the door hunched, looking at her. She didn't see the cooler.

"Cody, sit right here and don't move." She set him on the metal foldout chair and walked over. Jay-Jay leaned against a car, clutching his ribcage.

"What's wrong with you?" Phil asked.

"I ran into some barbed wire back there." He coughed and moved to the side to show her the cooler. Good. She still had her evidence, but the duct tape was missing from the lid.

"Did you bring any food with you?" Anthony shouted.

"Yeah," Phil said. "Where's the grub?"

Looking over, she saw Cody in Phil's lap. She almost rushed back until Cody leaned over and poked Anthony, who legitimately fell for What's-That-On-Your-Shirt. Phil and Cody both laughed.

Turning back, she said, "You looked inside, didn't you?" His wide eyes answered for him. She hushed her voice. "I don't have a lot of time to explain, but we're going to need a car. Do you have one?"

As he nodded, his eyes fell slightly shut. Something was definitely wrong with him. She looked down.

"Be careful," she said. "You're standing in a puddle of oil."

He slipped and collapsed to the floor.

"Somebody help," Vivian shouted and knelt next to him.

Cradling his head, she peeled back his sticky jacket to find a fist-sized hole in his shirt. Red smears covered her hands. He hadn't been standing in oil. Jay-Jay began coughing up more blood.

T ammy laid her head back on the pillow. After an hour of questioning, the cops finally cleared from her front yard. Bunch of jerks. It would've been great to see Miss Priss busted on the hood of a squad car. That might've knocked her back a peg.

Still, calling the police had been a bad idea. Vivian was blood, and that still counted for something. Maybe that's the reason she didn't tell the cops that her sister had run off with Anthony and his friends.

Besides, those boys had just finished their community service. They didn't need any more shit. She grabbed her phone from her nightstand. Anthony always hid at the junkyard when things got hot. Maybe she'd just give them a heads up to watch themselves.

Just outside her bedroom window, that damn dog barked louder.

"Will you shut up?" She pulled the curtain back and smacked the window. The pit-bull tried to dig underneath her fence. Nothing else moved out there. Of course. One of these days, she'd fix that dog for good.

Something scraped behind her. Was that someone in her bedroom doorway? The dog barked again. No, it was nothing. Just the darkness, mixed with too much booze.

"Tammy," a deep voice called out. "Where did Vivian go with my son?"

"Shit." She jumped up. This had to be the bastard her sister was running from. She snatched the Taser from the nightstand and snapped a warning arc of electricity.

"Get the fuck out of my house," she shouted. "Or I'll fry your ass."

"Tell me where she went." He stepped forward. "And I'll let you walk out of here."

"I'll scream."

"I wonder who will hear." He clicked something together in the darkness. Were they knives? "Your screams. Who will hear?"

Shit. He was right. No one would notice anything over that barking dog. Two kids had been shot to death down the street last week. No witnesses. Her only chance was to fry this nut case and get to her car.

Quickly, she stepped toward the bathroom. He leapt across the room. She zapped the Taser under his chin and dropped him.

Shoving past, she raced down the dark hallway. His footsteps gained on her. Somehow, he'd already gotten back up. Where could she go? The front door. No, it would take too long to unlock.

She barreled through the swinging kitchen doors and yanked the butcher knife from the block. In the glass of the microwave, his reflection moved behind her. She turned and stabbed with all her strength. He howled in pain. The knife stuck from his chest, buried to its handle in the bastard's heart.

"Serve's you right," she said.

His head snapped up.

Jesus H. Christ. His teeth looked like they'd been capped with sharpened bone fragments. He began clinking them together as he pulled the knife from his chest. Blood poured from the wound. She wanted to run, but her legs wouldn't move. Slivers of light through the backyard blinds showed the corners of his mouth had ripped.

"I like that fire in your belly." His neck twitched. "What do you say we let it out?"

He swiped at her. She fell back against the stove and looked down. Her shirt had been ripped away. Four long gashes in her stomach leaked blood. The pain buckled her legs.

"Help—" She could barely scream.

"That's it." He snatched her arm and sat her at the kitchen table. "Let it out."

"I don't know where—" She couldn't breathe. "I didn't see where."

"My car's still in front." He punched the table. "Don't lie to me again."

Should she tell the truth? No. Couldn't turn this monster loose on Anthony. Vivian had the kid with her.

"Told you." She clutched her stomach. "She ran off."

"If you don't know anything, you're not much use to me. Are you?"

"Wait."

"I'll let Vivian know what a loyal sister she had," he said.

Tammy threw herself to the floor and snatched the knife. Something stabbed the base of her skull, and her body went limp. She couldn't move. Her legs. Her arms. Nothing.

"That should stop your kicking," he said.

His snort might have been laughter.

4

"Get over here." Vivian's shout echoed across the warehouse. Though he was unconscious, Jay-Jay jerked as she put pressure on his wound. She couldn't bear to look at the blood leaking between her fingers. No matter how this ended, she would have a lifetime to feel guilt. Tonight, she had to be strong, mechanical even.

Anthony ran up. Phil followed close behind carrying Cody. Outside, rain pelted the metal rooftop. They couldn't risk taking him into the storm. The paramedics needed to come here.

"Close that door." She pulled him away from the raindrops that splashed onto his face.

"Shit." Anthony held his hands to the sides of his head. He began pacing back and forth. "What the fuck are we going to do?"

"We need to get him to the hospital," she said. Both boys just stood there. "We need a phone. Do you have one?"

"I left mine at home," Phil said.

Jay-Jay coughed and then shivered. Though she hated the idea of moving him next to a blaze of toxic chemicals, there wasn't a choice.

"He needs to be warm," she said. "Help me move him."

Phil set Cody down. Grabbing Jay-Jay's arms and legs, they awkwardly carried him next to the fire. She knelt and put pressure on his side again.

"Get away from him," Anthony said.

"Hey." Phil grabbed his shoulder. "Just calm down."

"She doesn't know what she's doing." He slapped his hand away. "She's going to kill him."

"We don't have time for this," she said. "I need towels."

"I told you to get away from him."

From the corner of her eye, she saw Anthony move toward her. Pushing Cody behind her, she jumped up and faced him. Luckily, he was shorter than most men. They stood eye-to-eye.

"He is going to die if you don't quit your bullshit," she said.

"None of this would be happening if it wasn't for you."

For a moment, he looked like he would hit her. Then he stared down at Jay-Jay, and tried to blink away his tears.

Now, despite the razor blade tattoo on his neck, the attitude and spiked clothing, he looked too young to be here.

"It is my fault." Her voice shook. "And god, I'm so sorry, but please help me. We have to stop the bleeding."

His face softened. He wiped his eyes and said, "I've seen towels on the second floor before."

"Go. I need a first aid kit, too. And scissors."

He ran off. Seconds later, glass shattered upstairs. She turned to Phil. "Do either of you own a vehicle?"

"My car is down the street from your sister's house."

"Get it and come back. Don't let the police see you." She didn't want to give him the opportunity to argue, so she turned and knelt back down. "Go now."

Phil turned just as Anthony ran down the staircase. He handed her a stack of white towels, professionally cleaned and bundled. Then he gave her a first aid kit. Behind them, the metal door screeched open and then shut.

"Scissors?" she asked.

"It's all I could find." He handed her a rusted X-Acto blade.

"It'll do. Now, spread the towels out on the ground." He did, and then they both moved Jay-Jay off the oil-stained concrete. Leaning over, she whispered, "Stay with us."

Cody touched his cheek.

"Baby, he's going to be fine." She held him back. "He needs space."

"No," Cody said. "It's too late."

"I promise, I'll fix it. Now go sit down. And don't look over here."

He moved next to the fire and sat in the folding chair that faced away from her. She sliced the bloody shirt down the center with the blade. Peeling it back, she gagged. Just below his ribs, a fist-sized crater had been torn from his side. Five claw marks surrounded the edges.

"Fuck me." Anthony stepped back.

"Mommy."

"Turn around." She pointed at Cody. "Now."

Originally she thought that Jarod's people had hurt Jay-Jay. Now she knew the severed hand was responsible. When she'd seen the thing earlier, it hadn't been that mobile. He must have brought it close enough to latch on.

"Keep your feet off of the floor," she said to Cody, just in case. He scrunched up his knees.

After dabbing blood from the wound, she grabbed one of the bleached towels and taped it to Jay-Jay's chest. When finished, she covered him with the rest of them.

"What's going on?" Anthony returned with his arms folded. "Is he going to live?"

Jay-Jay's breathing seemed strong considering. And he was young. All of this played in his favor. Still, she couldn't take her eyes from the trail of blood that led from the front door.

"Phil really needs to hurry," she said. "Was there a phone in the office?"

"There's no dial tone."

She sat in a chair next to the fire, her hands sticky with blood. With her sleeve, she wiped her forehead. All they could do now was wait. When Phil arrived, the two boys could take Jay-Jay to the hospital, and she would split off with Cody.

Hold on—

"Where's Cody?" she asked. Anthony looked around. Sharp objects filled every inch of the garage. And that hand could be anywhere.

"Baby." She raced behind some type of drill press. "Where are you?"

A faint giggle somewhere in the distance.

"Cody," Anthony shouted.

"Shhh." She waved at him. "Don't move."

He stopped, leaving only sound of rain. Something scraped above them.

"Where are the stairs?" she asked.

"You have to walk behind the pickup to see them."

"Stay with Jay-Jay," she said. "I'll get him."

She felt her way to the stairs in near darkness and raced up. At the top, a suspended catwalk led to a doorway. Light crept underneath.

Cody said something, but she couldn't make out the words. She ran down the hall and shoved the door open. Her stomach dropped. He sat alone on his knees, rocking back and forth in front of a desk. In his left hand, he held the razor blade that she'd used to cut Jay-Jay's shirt. His eyes were open, but they had rolled back to show only white.

"No." He held up the knife, and said to the wall. "I won't do that again."

The lamp on the desk buzzed brighter. She could have sworn it was hotter, too. Shadows moved across the walls, until the light popped into complete darkness.

8

Vivian didn't dare breathe. With the blade in Cody's hand, she couldn't move to him. What if she tripped? She couldn't shake the image of her baby bleeding in her arms. Through the only window, electricity cracked the sky. Briefly, the light showed Cody's position. She raced over and pulled the knife from his hand.

"Cody," she whispered in his ear. "It's okay. Mommy's here."

"No." He pulled away. The darkness returned. "I don't want to do it."

"Baby, we have to go."

Outside, more veins of lightning branched dangerously close to the metal warehouse. With his eyes rolled back, he reached for the window. Again darkness.

"Killing twelve early this morning," a thin voice called out.

Just feet away, a radio had turned on. It dialed through the stations. Celine Dion melded into La Bamba, until only a gentle shushing sounded. Whispers came through the static first. Then children's voices, dozens of them, chanting and giggling.

"Screw this." She picked up Cody.

The voices from the radio grew angry, hissing against her eardrum.

"Ring a ring a roses," Cody said. Neither his voice nor his rigid body possessed the playground innocence of the rhyme. "Pocket full of posies. Ashes. Ashes."

Trailing one hand on the wall for guidance, she found the door and raced down the catwalk.

"We all fall down," he said.

"Everything's going to be okay." Carefully, she descended the stairs into the dim light of the trash can fire.

"We all fall down," he repeated between frantic breaths. She choked back her tears when she saw that his eyes were still white.

"You found him," Anthony said as she ran up. He was sitting on a chair next to Jay-Jay.

"We need to get out of here," she said.

"What about Jay-Jay?"

"We'll carry him."

"In the rain? You said he could die."

For a moment, she considered telling him about Jarod's hand, about Cody and the radio. He already thought she was crazy though. Maybe she was, but every tingling hair on her body told her it was time to go.

"Somebody was upstairs with me," she said. "We're not alone here."

"What do you mean? I was just up there, and nobody's come in."

"We all fall down," Cody said.

Anthony pointed. "What the hell's wrong with him?"

She held Cody's face against her shoulder. "It's just something we sing when he's nervous. Now we need to go."

"Those government pigs are probably still out there," Anthony said. "People that you brought down on us. We can't take Jay-Jay out there."

"Listen, I don't care if you believe me or not. Somebody or something is upstairs right now."

"Something, huh?" Anthony rolled his eyes. "You're not taking Jay-Jay anywhere. I won't let you."

"London's burning," Cody said over her shoulder. "London's burning. Fetch the engine."

"Can't you get him to stop?" Anthony asked. "He's creeping me out."

She sat down in a chair and held Cody in her lap. Pushing sweaty strands of hair from his forehead, she said, "Baby, please wake up."

She shook him gently. A massive thunder strike rattled the building. The warehouse's metal beams moaned like a collapsing submarine. Cody breathed quicker. More than ever, she knew it was all connected. Jarod's deformation. The storm and Cody. Finally, she couldn't take it. She shook him harder and shouted, "Wake up."

An explosion above. Dozens of windows that lined the warehouse's ceiling imploded. She dove to the concrete and smothered Cody. Shards of glass sprayed down. Luckily, they were near the center of the building. Wind and rain poured through the windows now. Trash blew everywhere.

"Christ." Anthony pointed at Cody. He started to back away from them. "It's him. He's doing this."

He ran to the steel doors, pulled them open, and disappeared outside. She couldn't worry about him now. At this point, he wouldn't be much help.

"I'm sorry, baby." She slapped Cody's face to wake him. The second time, his blue eyes rolled back. Immediately, the storm seemed to die down.

"Ouch." He rubbed the side of his face.

"You scared me." She hugged him tight. Though she wanted to end it there, it couldn't wait. "Who were you talking to?"

"He wants to come in again," Cody said.

"Who does? Who wants to come in?"

Before he could answer, the door squealed open. Phil ran up with a giant blanket folded under his arm.

"Oh, thank God," she said. "I was beginning to think you weren't going to make it."

"I told you my car was parked all the way back on K Street."

"I'm sorry. We need to leave. Did you see any police at Tammy's house?"

"No, but her front door was wide open."

Jay-Jay's skin color was pretty good considering. For the first time tonight, she felt as though they might actually get out of this.

"Where's Anthony?" Phil asked.

"He went for help, too." She couldn't be sure how Phil would react if he knew the truth of the night's events. The front door opened again.

"He's back," Phil said.

She looked up to see Anthony's bald head peek into the warehouse. Did he have a change of heart? No, he'd probably come back for his friends. Time for damage control. She needed to convince him that he hadn't seen anything unusual. That shouldn't be too hard considering the story.

"Use the blanket," she said to Phil. "We'll carry Jay-Jay on that."

A wet thudding sound filled her ears. Anthony's head rolled face up at her feet. Spattered in blood, his expression had frozen in terror. Skin hung from his neck from where it had been torn off.

"Cody." She snatched him up and covered his eyes.

Phil looked as though he knew what he was seeing, but couldn't process it.

"Vivian," Jarod growled from the shadows. "You've been a bad girl."

9

R un," Vivian shouted at Phil. Clutching Cody, she bolted to the back of the warehouse and stopped. The stairs and catwalk dead-ended with only a second-story window for escape. Instead, she raced along the drill presses and welding machines that lined the back wall. There had to be another exit.

"You're going to die," Phil yelled.

She ducked against the skeleton of a stripped car and peeked out. Phil raised a crowbar and squared off with Jarod. God, he needed to run.

"Did you hear that, Vivian?" Jarod's voice sounded amplified. Though he stood in darkness next to a suspended engine block, those teeth were unmistakable in the trashcan's firelight. "Your boyfriend here's upset with me."

"Fuck you." Phil charged him.

She ducked back. Metal clanged on the concrete, followed by a scream so intense that it seemed to chill the darkness around her. She covered Cody's ears too late. He whimpered.

"It's okay. Everything's going to be okay." She blinked back her tears. "Mommy loves you."

Jarod would never let her out of here alive. Somehow, that bastard had to die tonight. The guns. They were still inside the cooler behind him. She had to lure him away.

Lifting Cody into the front seat of the car chassis, she whispered, "Don't move. I'll be right back."

"No." He clutched her shirt.

"I promise I'm coming back."

"You can't breathe."

He was right. Her chest wheezed, and she'd left her inhalers back at the cabin. Saint Mary's was two blocks away. They could still make it, but she had to hurry.

"It's going to be fine." She gave her best smile and kissed his forehead. "Now don't move, no matter what you hear."

"Butterfly," Jarod called out. "I know you're there."

"Don't go." Cody shook his head. "Don't go."

"Shhh." She pulled a tarp on the front seat over him. "I love you."

"Butterfly." Jarod dragged out the word.

On the ground, she found a lug nut and tossed it through an upstairs window. In two agile moves, he leapt impossibly far into the shadows. Seconds later, it sounded as though he was tearing the upstairs office apart.

She raced for the cooler. Gurgled breaths. Jesus, Phil lay on the floor. His torso had been sheered vertically from the side of his neck to his stomach. Wide-eyed, he smeared a puddle of blood as he reached for her. She covered her mouth and looked away.

Then she crept over to the chest, peeled back the lid, and grabbed one of the guns.

"I wouldn't," Jarod said. She spun to find him towering over her. His sunken eyes looked starved, his cheeks torn like bloody rags. "I'll have your spine before you clear the first chamber."

"Please don't do this." She didn't know why she was trying to reason with him, except that somewhere inside this thing had to be Cody's father.

"Pleading," he said. "I like that."

"He's our son. Doesn't that mean anything to you?"

"You were the one who left me. Remember?"

"You broke Cody's ribs. You punctured his lung."

"Yes I did." With one bone claw, he gouged the fender of the car next to him. His other amputated arm trembled in spasms as he sliced the metal. "You want to know how that feels?"

"Daddy, stop it," Cody yelled across the warehouse.

Jarod's neck snapped to the side, right to the car where Cody was hidden. It was now or never. That son of a bitch would never take her baby. She grabbed the gun, swung the barrel up, and pulled the trigger. Bullets punched his chest, again and again, dancing him backwards until the gun chamber clicked empty. He collapsed to the ground.

Was he dead? Nothing could live through that. Yeah, nothing human. Where was that other gun? She grabbed it from the ice chest, stood over Jarod, and fired repeatedly into his head.

Chunks of skin, bone, and gore tore away, until the final round left his face unrecognizable. Leaning against the truck's grill, she tried not to look at the bloody mess. Cody cried hysterically across the room. She dropped the gun, ran back to the car, and pulled away the tarp.

"It's all over." She hugged him and kissed his tears. "He can't hurt us anymore."

Her muscles ached as she picked Cody up. Careful to hold his face away from the bodies, she staggered to the sliding front door and screeched it open.

Outside, streaks of sunlight pierced the storm clouds. What did this all mean? Nothing. Jarod was dead, but his crazy family was still out there. If life had taught her anything, it was that people who got their hopes up were asking to get kicked. She needed to stay focused.

"Close it." Cody pointed at the front door. "Don't leave me with him."

"It's okay now," she said. Her chest grew tighter. Her asthma was kicking in hard now, but there was still time to make it to the hospital. Sparks popped in her vision. "We're going to the doctor. Everything is going to be okay."

"No it's not."

Dizzy and exhausted, she slammed the door shut, found a pole, and rammed it through the handles to lock it.

"See," she said. "He can't get us anymore."

The door rattled. She jumped back. It couldn't be. She'd almost blown his head off. Four claws slammed through the door and sheared it. She turned to run, but her legs collapsed. She managed to set Cody down before she face-planted into a huge puddle. Wiping her eyes, she coughed a mouthful of gritty water. Cody stood alongside her, pulling her shirt as she crawled.

"Leave," she tried to shout at him, but the words choked in her throat. Jarod punched his way through the door.

"Run." She gasped. "Please, baby. Just run."

"Mommy."

"I'm right—" She paused for breath. "—behind you."

Jarod walked toward them. Chunks of his scalp were still missing, but worms of flesh on his skull appeared to fuse and heal before her eyes. She urged Cody to run, but he just stood crying.

Sunlight reflected over the top of the warehouse, blinding her. Her breaths grew shallow. Then Jarod stood above her.

"I want you to see this before you choke to death." He snatched the back of Cody's pajamas with that claw. Her vision constricted as she reached for her baby.

"Don't hurt him," she shouted.

"Mommy." Cody reached back with both arms.

Tears filled her eyes as she listened to him scream. Jarod dragged him away by his shirt. Desperately, she tried to chase them, but her body wouldn't move. And then she could see only a blurred sky. Darkness.

II

DESPERATION

10

J arod woke with a throbbing headache. Looking down in
the dark, he found his body covered in...what was that?
Mud? A rotting smell stuck to the back of his throat.
Somewhere across the room, a fly buzzed against a
windowpane. He felt around, found a light on the bed
stand, and clicked it on. A smeared handprint across the
lamp's shade doused the room with reddish glow.

"Shit." He jumped onto the cold concrete floor and
nearly slipped. Pools of blood stained the white sheets. He
looked down. This couldn't be happening. His forearm had
been severed. Rough scar tissue capped the injury.
Someone must have kidnapped him. The bastards had cut
off his arm. For what? Proof of life. They took his arm! He
needed a phone. Rankin would handle this. Whoever did it
was fucking dead.

"It's been awhile." A raspy voice made him jump. "Twenty-seven years. Come to think, it'll be twenty-eight next week."

Next to a guitar and amp on the far side of the room, a black man creaked back and forth in a rocking chair. His uneven gray Afro spilled into an equally scraggly beard. His eyes were simultaneously kind and disturbing, as if he were some old blues singer sitting in front of a bloodbath, waiting patiently for his next gig in hell.

"No matter how much money you get from my people, it won't save you. Your children won't recognize you when I'm finished."

"I hope you're not blaming me for last night." The man pointed a knobby finger at him. His varicose hands looked ancient. Jarod didn't see any weapons.

"If you didn't do it, who did?"

"That's not important right now—"

"Answer me," he said loudly. "Who took my arm?"

The man stopped rocking. The room grew cold.

"I've watched out for your family for a long time now," he said. "But I *can* leave."

"Conrad," a woman's muffled voice called out. "What's going on down there?"

Jarod spun to find a wooden staircase leading up. Across the room, the only window had no bars. This was no cell. It looked like a basement that had been converted to a bedroom. That didn't make sense. If he wasn't being held hostage, what was happening? The blood. His arm.

"Talk quiet," the old man whispered. "This is Janet Winston's house. You broke in here last night when you ran out of the juice. Trust me, you don't want that woman coming down and finding out what you did to her son in the bathroom over there."

Just then, Jarod noticed the blood trail that led into the darkness beside the old man.

"Conrad," she repeated. Above, a door opened. Jarod stepped back from the light that spilled down the staircase. "We didn't let you move back in so that you could sleep all day." She paused. "I swear."

The door slammed. Footsteps thumped away.

"Who the hell are you?" Jarod turned back.

"Just an old friend. Here to help you through a difficult situation."

"Your name now or I promise—"

"I am Mister Vincent."

Jarod felt dizzy. That name. Where had he heard it before?

"What happened to me?" he asked. "My arm?"

"You tangled with the wrong alley cat last night." Mister Vincent chuckled. "That Vivian is quite a lady."

Vivian. His stomach burned with anger. That's right. He'd found her hiding in Mercer. But then what? His memory blurred. It didn't matter. He should've known that bitch was somehow responsible for this. If she was on the move again, there'd be a trail for Rankin to follow. A cell phone sat on the end table. He walked over and picked it up. Before this day ended, he'd personally beat the life from her.

"Put it down," Mister Vincent said. "You're not going to touch her. Besides, the police aren't going to think too highly of this situation when they show up."

"They'll do what they're told, or they'll end up with her."

"Use your head. Cody's not going to react well if you kill his mother. Your boy already sees too much. It's dangerous. And foolish."

He started to dial Rankin's number with his left hand, and was reminded of his arm again. She'd turned him into some kind of freak. For that, he'd make her beg for death.

"You're insane if you think she's going to get away with this," Jarod said.

"You're calling me crazy?"

"Nuts."

"If I'm so crazy, then why are you the one who's chatting with himself?"

Jarod looked up to find the basement empty. He spun around, but he was alone with his thundering heart.

Above, the door opened again.

"Conrad." A heavy-set woman clomped down the stairs, fiddling with a set of keys. "I told you the dishes in the washer were clean."

She reached the bottom, glanced up, and froze.

"Take anything you want." She stepped back, and then looked at the bed's bloody sheets. "Oh God."

She darted upstairs. He leapt forward and grabbed her ankle. She slammed into the staircase, and her body fell to the floor below.

"Please," she said as he spun her over. "Don't."

What could he do? His fingerprints would be everywhere. And she could ID him. A thought crept into his head. She could've slipped while trying to escape a house fire. The fumes could have overcome her.

"Whatever it is that you're thinking," Mister Vincent said. "I can promise you that it's not smart."

From the corner of his eye, he saw the old man standing a few feet away now. His posture seemed tense, like a stalking predator.

"Get out of my head."

"Pull yourself together," Mister Vincent said. "Change your clothes. Tie her up in the yard and burn the house. You'll be fine."

"She's seen my face."

"I won't tell anyone," the woman mumbled through a swollen lip.

"She can't touch you," Mister Vincent said.

"No," Jarod told him. "I won't take the chance."

"Don't let your son see you behaving this way. Too much is at stake."

"He'll never know."

"He's here right now. Don't you remember?"

Just then, a sound came from across the room. He kept an eye on the woman as he walked over and opened the closet door. Cody hid in the back corner, under the hanging clothes. Finally. His luck had changed. The bitch had taken his arm, but he'd taken more from her. He didn't need to look for her. Vivian would come to him now.

"Mister Vincent." Cody stared over Jarod's shoulder.

"What did you say?" Jarod looked back to see the old man behind him. "You can see him?"

Did that mean Mister Vincent was real? Even a family of lunatics couldn't share the exact same delusion.

"Keep it together," Mister Vincent said. "For your boy's sake."

What could he do? Vivian had taken his arm. There was no way in hell he would let her live. Still, he couldn't shake the fear in his gut. For now, he needed to play along. At least until he figured out what was going on.

"What do I need to do?" he asked.

11

Vivian woke drenched in sweat. Her throat felt raw. To the left, a heart monitor beeped incessantly. Glancing around, she found herself lying on a gurney, dressed in only a hospital gown. That thing had her baby!

She shot up in bed. A hollow clink pulled at her arm. One of her hands was cuffed to the guardrail. She yanked an IV from the top of her wrist and tried to squeeze through the restraint. It was too tight.

Jarod wouldn't hurt Cody. But he wasn't himself. Somehow, she had to get out of here.

The door next to her hospital bed opened. A white-haired man walked from the bathroom.

"Wonderful. You're awake." He dried his hands with a paper towel. Was he police? Maybe, but weren't cops supposed to retire before sixty? And they didn't wear expensive suits. "I trust that you're comfortable," he said.

His courteous, British accent seemed out of place with his icy stare.

"I'm fine." Did they know who she was yet? She never carried identification. Still, they only needed her fingerprints, and it would be over. "Can you loosen this handcuff? My arm is numb."

"I'm afraid I can't do that," he said. "I've seen many things in my day, young lady, but I have never seen anything like the mess you left at the scrap yard."

"Mess?" She paused to calm her voice. Those boys had given their lives to protect Cody, but to this jerk they were little more than a cleanup on aisle four. "You think I killed them?"

"I don't suppose it was you, but you do know who is responsible."

"I never got a look at him." As far as she was concerned, everyone worked for Jarod. Especially the police. "Why am I handcuffed then? I've done nothing wrong."

"We can't be sure of that until you answer some questions."

He looked at her, then down at her scraped thigh. The hospital gown felt inadequate. She pulled it down with her free hand.

"Now." He walked over to a chair, grabbed a folded blanket, and handed it to her. "You were telling me of last night's events."

She unfolded the blanket slowly to buy time. What could she possibly tell him? That one of the most powerful men in California was actually some kind of, thing…she didn't even know what the hell he was. As usual, her best bet was to shut her mouth and handle the problem herself.

"I didn't see him," she said.

"Do you expect me to believe that those boys were murdered in front of you, and you saw nothing?"

"It was dark."

"Protecting a murderer makes you an accomplice to his crimes. Not only that, but—"

"Protecting somebody who tried to kill me? Someone who left me to die? That makes a ton of sense."

His jaw muscles clenched. "You should never interrupt somebody when they are speaking."

"I'm sorry." Her temper wasn't going to help this situation. "I told you that I didn't see him. There's nothing more to say." She rattled the cuff against the railing. "Now please, I need to go to the bathroom."

"Very well," he said. "Silence is always the wisest choice."

"What?"

"Vivian," he said. Her stomach dropped. "Because you're able to keep a secret, I'll let you in on another one. I'm not really a detective. My name is Stromsky."

Hairs stood on her neck. When they were married, Jarod had always seemed in control, confident. Except when he mentioned Kevin Stromsky's name.

"You work for the Ronan-Carmichael Foundation," she said.

"Your husband has spoken of me?" His eyes narrowed. "To you?"

She shouldn't have said anything.

"I just know you," she said. "Your name, I mean, from the website."

"Ah." He smiled, showing teeth that were far too white. "Since you know my name, perhaps it's time you understood what I do for the foundation."

He walked over to the blinds and closed them. She realized that she'd seen no doctors, nurses, nor any other patients for that matter.

"From time to time, even charitable organizations can suffer from certain political stains." He wiped his hands on his suit coat, as if the mention of it had soiled them. "It is my job to keep such business from tarnishing the Carmichael family name. Do you know why I'm trusted for such an important task? Even at my age?"

"Just listen to me," she said. "I don't know anything."

"I am preferred because no matter how filthy or unspeakable the mess, I always leave a spotless shine."

"I only want my son. Your problems have nothing to do with me."

"Now that's where we disagree," he said. "Let me paint two scenarios. The first involves you staying quiet. The family stays happy, and I don't have to wet my hands."

"I only want my son," she repeated.

"I can see we're not communicating." He reached up and slid the privacy curtain around her bed.

"I'll scream."

Instantly, he leapt forward. With one hand, he clamped her throat and slammed her head back into her pillow. She tried to punch him, but he grabbed her wrist and bent it forward. Pain crippled her. He leaned in close and stared into her eyes.

"The only reason that you're alive," he said. "Is because a boy should not grow up without his mother." He released his grip. Gasping for air, she leaned over the edge of the bed. "I trust we won't need to discuss these matters again." He pulled a packet from his side pocket, opened it, and began scrubbing his fingernails with a handy wipe.

"What do you want from me?" She coughed violently.

"If I may be honest, the family never approved of your marriage. Given your background, you can understand why. Now, however, it seems now that young Cody represents the best hope to carry on the Carmichael legacy."

"What are you talking about?" The thought of Cody growing up to be one of those people sickened her. "There are others. Frederick. Casey."

"A bastard and an autistic. No, they simply won't do. For now, the burden rests on your shoulders. You will raise Cody. Focus on his studies and athletics."

"Jarod will kill me."

"Ah, yes." He reached into his jacket pocket with the wet napkin, pulled out a hooked bone claw, and set it on the tray next to her. "I think the situation has changed, wouldn't you agree?"

"You saw what happened last night?"

"I don't know what I witnessed."

From the look on his face, she could tell he didn't want to know either.

"That man behaves like a filthy street thug. You can imagine the predicament this puts the family in."

Could Jarod's twisted family be on her side in all of this? Still, she couldn't help her apprehension. Bargains with the devil were easy. It was the payment that presented the problem.

"What do you want from me?" she asked.

"You're going to help us put him down quietly."

"What? Me? I don't know how to do that."

"Believe me when I say that this is not a request." He leaned over and unlocked her handcuff. "You're to go to the estate tonight and get your son. Do as we ask Vivian, and Cody will be back in your arms soon."

"Wait," she said.

"You'll find some new clothes in the rest room. A cell phone, too." He walked across the room to the door. "I'll be in touch."

Then he left her alone. Immediately, she raced to the bathroom to dress. Screw that bastard. She'd get Cody back tonight. And this time, they'd disappear into a rainforest so thick that the mosquitoes would have trouble breathing.

She opened the bathroom door and gasped. On the closed toilet lid, a burly police officer sat in full uniform. He stared at the wall in front of him with lifeless eyes. A wire-thin bruise line stretched across his neck. He'd probably been the actual officer assigned to watch her.

Stromsky had just strangled this man while she slept in the next room.

12

J arod dragged Cody by his hand, down the driveway to the minivan parked on the curb. Thunderclouds darkened the sky. Palm trees swayed in the humid wind, but he couldn't find any street signs or recognizable landmarks.

Whatever city this was didn't matter. He needed to get out of here. Vivian had turned him into a freak show attraction that could be picked from any lineup. Once he found his way home, Rankin would dispose of the car. Then he would deal with her.

"Mister Vincent," Cody shouted.

"You'd better quit." Jarod snatched his collar. "He can't help you."

Vincent, whatever the hell he was, had been absent ever since Jarod had changed out of the bloody clothes.

"What's going on out there?" A neighbor opened her screen door. She hobbled down her walkway, wearing only a nightgown. Wisps of her silver hair blew every direction in the windstorm.

"Help," Cody shouted.

"Go back inside," Jarod said to the woman. Then he opened the van's sliding rear door. "Everything's fine."

"He doesn't sound fine," she said. Raindrops began dotting the sidewalk. The old woman opened her front gate and walked toward them.

With his good arm, he picked up Cody, who latched onto the van as he tried to put him into the backseat. They didn't have time for this. Any moment the gas could ignite, and this woman looked like she had nothing better to do than dial nine-one-one.

"Where are you going with the Winston's van?" She looked around, probably to see if other neighbors were nearby. None were.

Jarod shoved Cody inside the car, closed the door, and turned around. "Mind your own business."

"Help me." Cody slapped the window.

Suddenly, glass shattered. Fire erupted from the windows of the Winston's house. The unlit oven burners had ignited too soon.

"Oh my God," the woman said.

Flames started consuming the house, but her eyes never strayed from him. He raced to the driver's side, got in, and sped away. What the hell was he thinking leaving witnesses behind? Especially on the advice of a hallucination. He should've killed the old woman. The owner of the house too, instead of tying her up in the backyard. Now, he was in a stolen vehicle with the police on their way. Could this get any worse?

Ahead, he saw the Devonshire onramp to I-405 north. Finally, a break. They were still in California. By the time the police caught any scent, he'd already be safe at the estate. Safe. What a joke. He studied the twisted scar mesh on his forearm.

"Tell me what you know about Mister Vincent." He tipped down the rear view mirror. Cody looked away. "You will answer me."

"You hurt Mommy," he said quietly.

Could that be true? God he hoped so. He'd given her everything. Made her somebody. Worked his ass off for her. Only to have that bitch cut off his arm.

"Your mother stole you from your family." The rain picked up. He turned on the wipers, which smeared dirty rainwater across the windshield. "What she did was wrong."

"You'd better not hurt her again. Mister Vincent will be mad."

Was that a threat? No. He was only four. He didn't understand what was going on.

"I'll take my chances," Jarod said.

"He'll chop off your leg."

"What did you say?" In the mirror, Cody's blue eyes stood out against his pale skin. His own son looked back with anger. "Come up here."

Cody jumped to the very back seat. Jarod clinched the steering wheel. Vivian would pay for brainwashing his son.

"We'll be home soon," Jarod said. "And Mister Vincent won't be able to save you then. Or your mother."

"You better be good."

His gut clenched. Wait. He wanted to know about Vincent. Outsmarting a four-year-old shouldn't be that hard.

"I don't think Mister Vincent is coming back."

"He always does."

"Where is he then?"

"Cody Town."

"Bring him here," Jarod said. "I want to talk to him." Cody didn't seem to know how to respond. "Do it now or else I'll find your mother and hurt her."

"Bad Daddy."

The car stereo screeched to life, dialing through the stations. He pushed the buttons to no effect. "You'd better not hurt her again."

"Quit it," Jarod shouted over the radio, which blared so loudly that his ears hurt.

Something dripped on his shirt. He pulled down the rear view mirror and saw a stream of blood pouring from his nose. Sores and pustules began sprouting on his face. He grabbed a dirty rag from the passenger seat and tried to stop the flow of blood.

"Bad Daddy."

"Dammit," he shouted. "Quit it."

Was Cody really doing this? It had to be him.

"Bad," Cody said.

Jarod swerved to the side of the road. An old Ford Taurus directly behind him fishtailed. He pulled to a stop and undid his seatbelt.

"Stop this," Jarod shouted. "I'm sorry I lost my temper."

A migraine nearly crippled him as he staggered to the back.

"Listen to me." He took hold of Cody. His teeth began popping in his mouth and falling out.

"You're bad," Cody said. A bitter chill turned the cab into a meat locker. Ice crystals formed at the base of the windows and began growing up the sides.

"I'll find your mother and help her. I swear it."

"He's sorry." Cody's shallow breaths fogged on contact with the freezing air. "He promised he won't hurt her."

"I promise," he shouted.

"He really means it this time. Stop it."

Instantly, everything returned to normal. No blood on his shirt. He felt his face. No sores either. What had just happened? More fucking mind games. No, that had been the most intense headache he'd ever felt. Worse than that, ice crystals still covered the windows.

"What was that?" he demanded.

"Mister Vincent said he's watching you. You'd better be good, Daddy."

"Tell him I will." Jarod leaned back against the sliding door and wiped the cold sweat from his forehead. "I will."

Mister Vincent had done that as a warning. For what? To protect Vivian? He stared at his severed forearm. There's no way he'd let her live. Not after all she'd taken from him.

For now though, he needed to stay calm. When he figured out what was going on, then he would strike. And if Mister Vincent stood in his way, Mister Vincent would die, too. It didn't matter what he was. Everything could be killed if you knew where to stab.

He moved back to the driver's seat and then pulled onto the freeway. Vivian would come for Cody soon. He had to be ready.

13

Under gray thunderclouds, dozens of statues guarded Saint Lucia Cathedral and its connected graveyard. Some angelic sculptures seemed to protect the dead with prayer, while others were of the Old Testament variety with swords in hand. Vivian prayed for assistance from the latter. Forgiveness would be no part of the plan to get Cody back tonight.

Staring at her mother's grave, she couldn't shake her guilt. All her life, she'd promised that she'd be a better mother than her own. Now, the string of drunken boyfriends and parties seemed far better by comparison. She felt like screaming at somebody, anybody, but there was nobody to blame but herself.

Something splashed behind her. She turned. A blue Prius pulled up alongside the stone church. Erika opened the door, stood from the car, and smiled. Kinky, reddish-brown curls replaced her trademark long braids.

"Girl, you have got to calm down on the Jason Bourne shit. You're wearing a sister out." She laughed, walked up, and they hugged.

"It's for your own good."

"Please." She flashed an uncaring look and primped her hair. "I know you like to think I need protection, but I can take care of myself."

"Jarod found us. He has Cody."

"Oh God." Erika held her hand to her chest. "What are we going to do?"

"He won't hurt him. I know he won't hurt him." She pushed the thought of those torn cheeks aside. The claws. If she focused on anything but the plan, she'd fall apart. "I'm getting him back tonight. I just need your help with a few things. Then pretend you never heard from me."

"You must be kidding."

"Did you bring it?" Vivian asked.

"In the back, and don't change the subject."

She walked over to the car's hatch, opened it, and grabbed the shovel.

"Hold up," Erika said from behind. "Do you really think that I'm going to sit on the sidelines?"

"You don't understand." She turned. How could she convey the real danger without sounding nuts? "Jarod killed three boys last night. He almost murdered me."

Erika looked horrified. She pulled out her cell from her purse. "We've got to call the police."

Vivian put her hand over the phone. "You know I can't do that."

"But I can. He's my godson. I'll call and say I'm concerned for his safety."

"If you do, they'll pin everything on me. They've done it before."

"You act like I'm not the one who picked you up from jail that night," she said.

"Then you know what Jarod can do. Cody was in intensive care, and every single one of those pigs covered for him. They said I was unfit."

"This is different. His fingerprints have to be at the crime scene. The evidence. This could be your chance to come out of hiding."

She knew better. Some mistakes you never stopped paying for. Especially the ones made when you were nineteen, and headstrong, and stupid. And yet she felt guilty thinking of her marriage like that, because Cody had come from it.

"We can't involve them," she said.

"Fine, we'll leave the police out of it, but that's only more reason that you need my help."

"We don't have time to argue."

Erika threw up her hands. "You have to be the most stubborn woman that I've ever known."

They approached her mom's grave in silence. Knuckled roots wove underneath the foundations of the statues. Vivian knelt and pulled away the overgrown weeds to find a headstone flush to the ground. She stood and punched the shovel into the grass.

"Don't tell me that your plan involves digging up your mom?" Erika asked.

A bitter wind swept down from the dark clouds, as if her words carried some curse.

"It's not what you think." She looked around to make sure they were alone. "I have to get my money."

"You buried it in your mom's grave?"

"I needed a safe landmark," Vivian said. Erika gave her a look. "It's not as if I could've opened a bank account with it."

"Hey, it's your life. All I'm saying is that's some serious bad mojo."

Gravel popped behind them. She looked back to find a golf cart pull up behind Erika's car. A middle-aged man got out and walked up to them. His maintenance uniform was cobwebbed and dirty. The cemetery's insignia was sewn into the chest.

"What the hell are you doing?" he asked.

Erika stepped between them and said, "You wouldn't happen to have another shovel, would you?"

Vivian used the distraction to continue digging.

"I'm calling the police," he said.

"Hold up." Erika followed him back to his cart.

The shovel hit something. Vivian knelt and brushed away the loose dirt. Thank God. The nylon duffle bag was still there. She grabbed the handles and pulled. After several attempts, the bag broke free. The groundskeeper drove away.

"We need to go," Erika said.

They walked over to the car, got in, and sped off. Approaching the gate to the cemetery, she saw the man talking to a coworker. He pointed at them as they passed.

"This just proves my point," Erika said. "You're going to need somebody to watch your back."

"You don't know these people. The things they're capable of."

"Cody is in the hands of a murderer." Erika's words seemed to steal the air from the car. "Are you going to send the one person who's on your side away?"

She was right. It was crazy to think she could take on Jarod alone. She'd need an army to get her baby away from the Carmichaels. Or at least anyone who wanted to help.

"If you go with me," Vivian said. "Please be careful. I don't know what I'd do if I lost you."

"Don't you worry about me. I'm a big girl." Erika turned onto Highway 101. "So where to?"

"I stashed this before I left him." She unzipped the duffle bag, tore open the black plastic inside, and showed the stacks of bank-bound hundreds. In the front pouch, passports and ID's. "I want to get in and out. This time, I'm going to have to leave the country."

Erika whistled. "That man won't see us coming."

Vivian wished that were true, but her hollow stomach told her otherwise. Would he still be that monster? And if he was, could he be killed? That didn't matter. Everything depended on her slipping into the estate, finding Cody, and disappearing without any contact. Still, she wasn't about to break into his guarded compound defenseless.

"What's the plan?" Erika asked.

"We get him back tonight, but we have to make a stop first. We need guns. Big ones."

14

Jarod raced around the corner onto Magnolia Street. For the last twenty miles, the roads had been relatively dark. Now as the minivan sped up the hill to the estate, rows of outdoor lights that lined the driveway pulsed in front of his eyes, making his head throb. He yanked down the visor.

They'd finally reached the estate, but he didn't feel safe. Not after waking up in a stranger's house covered in blood. And definitely not after Vincent's mind games earlier. Nothing seemed real anymore. In this whole mess, he knew only one thing. For whatever reason, Mister Vincent wanted Vivian alive. There was no way in hell.

"Are we going to find Mommy?" Cody asked from the back seat.

"Soon." He pressed the accelerator.

She'd come tonight. He knew it. Somehow, her death needed to look accidental. But how could he hide anything from Mister Vincent, a fucking demon? If he moved fast enough, it wouldn't matter. Once she was dead, Vincent's only option would be to forget it. That, or leave Cody orphaned. Something told Jarod that he wouldn't do that.

"When are we going to find her?" Cody asked.

"I said soon." He stopped at the guardhouse and rolled down his window. For the first time, the eight-foot wall surrounding the estate seemed inadequate. Leon exited the booth with his hand on his firearm.

"Just open the gate," Jarod said. A blinding light punched his eyes. "Get that off me or I swear to Christ—"

"Sorry, sir." The beam shut off. "I didn't recognize the vehicle."

"Open it."

Leon moved to the booth, hit a switch, and the gate moaned. Jarod drove through. Within minutes, he managed to carry Cody into the study without running into any other staff.

Though the wall candles were decorative, he lit them. Shadows and firelight stretched across the bookshelves.

"Sit," he told Cody, and then pushed the estate's intercom button. "I need David Rankin in the study."

Cody climbed onto the antique couch on the far side of the room. Using the remote, Jarod turned on the hanging television in the corner. He had to see if the police had any leads on the house fire.

He sat at his desk and did his best to conceal his arm. With Cody in the room, it wasn't time for them to discuss what Vivian had done. The double oak doors whooshed open.

"You're back." Rankin stormed inside. In the dim light, the birthmark covering his left eye seemed more sinister. His trench coat and slick hair were soaked.

"You look like hell," Jarod said.

"We caught a break while you were gone," Rankin said. "Your wife's sister contacted LAPD. We almost had Vivian in Los Reyes last night."

"That doesn't matter," Jarod said.

"If we move now, we can catch her."

"I told you that it doesn't matter." He pointed to Cody on the couch.

"You found him. Is she here too?" Rankin glanced around the room. His eyes came to rest on Jarod's severed arm. "What the hell happened?"

"I'm fine, but there isn't much time. She'll come for him tonight."

Rankin pulled his trench coat aside and grabbed the radio from his belt. "We need to lift you both to a secure location."

"Put that away," Jarod said. "We're staying here."

"T-Bar Ranch is secluded. I've already got men on standby."

"Good. Bring them here." He didn't know what kind of backlash to expect from Mister Vincent once he killed Vivian, but more security couldn't hurt.

"There are too many variables." Rankin kept his hand on his radio. "There's no way to really guard the back cliffs, the orchard is too dark and open, and she used to live here."

"That's what I'm counting on. When she comes, we'll be ready."

"You better be good," Cody said. "Mister Vincent's watching."

Jarod bit his tongue. His own son was a goddamn surveillance camera. If his plan was going to work, he couldn't tip his hand. Not to Rankin. Not to anyone without running the risk of Mister Vincent overhearing.

"I won't touch your mother," Jarod said, and then he turned to Rankin. "This ends tonight. Vivian and I are going to work everything out. Now get your men over here. I want the security alarms off. When she arrives, you're going to leave a path for her to find her way inside."

"What?" Rankin demanded. "She might bring a weapon."

"The woman hates guns."

"That wouldn't stop her from hiring someone. As your friend, I'm telling you that this is a bad idea."

"I think I can handle my own wife."

"Yeah," Rankin said. "I can see that."

"I think you've forgotten who you're talking to." He stood. For a brief moment, he felt the urge to gut the man. To stand over his broken body.

"Do I look like a security guard to you? You take off last night without telling anyone. You show up today as an amputee. It's my job to take the bullet that's calling your name. What the hell did you expect me to say?"

"I expect you to do your job." He grabbed his chair and sat back down at the desk. "I know what I'm doing."

"You hired me to protect your life. I take that seriously."

"I know. That's the only reason I'm going to forgive this incident. Now take my son to his room. We're not leaving."

Rankin didn't move for a second. Finally, he looked at Cody and said, "Let's go."

"There's just one more thing." Jarod motioned to Rankin, who walked close and leaned down. "If you ever speak to me like that in front of my son again," he said quietly. "I'll bury you in the rose garden."

 espes

Stromsky parked in darkness just outside of the Carmichael estate. So far, everything had fit the plan. Jarod had just arrived. Vivian was on her way. Perfect. His cellular phone rang.

He reached into his inner coat pocket and answered.

"Mrs. Carmichael on the line," her assistant said. "Please hold."

Though the man's tone was curt, and quite rude he might add, it didn't reflect on Charlotte. Good help was impossible to find these days.

"Kevin, darling." She finally came on the line. "It's been far too long."

"Charlotte, your company is always worth the wait."

"I take it that you've found my grandson."

"He's just arrived with his father now."

"I see." Her voice was unusually even. That could only mean one thing. The difficult decision of what to do with Jarod had been made.

"Shall I move?" he asked.

"My son has become a bit too much like his father. A liability to the Carmichael legacy."

"I understand," Stromsky said. *Dispose of Jarod discreetly.* "And what of Vivian?"

"A boy shouldn't be separated from his mother, but I fear that she's unstable and can't be trusted."

"I've already spoken with her this afternoon. She'll be arriving tonight."

"I don't need to tell you that appearances must be kept," she said. "My son should never have married that woman."

"I understand." A house fire would work well here, or perhaps a lovely automobile accident for the media to swoon over. Simple enough. "Your grandson will be in proper care by morning."

"Please call when you're finished, Kevin. We'll meet for tea. We must catch up."

"Until then, Charlotte."

16

Night had almost arrived when they passed mile marker fifty-seven. Erika slowed and turned off Highway 101 onto a dirt road. As they wound farther from cross traffic, Vivian grew uneasy. She wanted to avoid prying eyes, but this area seemed dangerously secluded. Still, nothing would stop her from getting Cody back tonight, and she couldn't risk running into Jarod without some protection.

"He should be here soon," Erika said as they reached a clearing. Under a dark and dirty sky, a lattice of rusted beams and walkways connected three decaying silos. "I hope you know what you're doing."

"You do know this guy, right?"

"Contrary to public opinion, most black folks don't have gun pushers on speed dial. He was our only option."

"Sorry." She realized how rude it sounded. "I'm just nervous."

"I know you're scared for Cody. I'm terrified too, but this feels wrong. Let's just leave."

"I can't go into the estate unarmed."

"I'll buy you anything you want from the store."

She'd already considered it, but the waiting period was out of the question.

"I'm getting him back tonight," Vivian said.

"Even if you had a gun, do you really think you can just slip by Jarod's security?"

"If you've got a better idea."

"With that much cash, I can think of a dozen. Hire somebody."

"Who?" Vivian asked. "I don't know those kinds of people, and he could always pay them more."

Brakes squealed behind them. To the left, a dark sedan pulled into the lot. It parked about thirty yards away.

"We can still leave," Erika said.

"I can't." She tucked a single stack of hundreds underneath her belt. Ten thousand should cover anything she needed. "Hang here in case something goes wrong."

"Fine, but if we end up in a dumpster, it's on you."

As she got out of the car, drizzled wind pushed against her. In the distance, a squeaking windmill formed an eerie rhythm with a piece of flapping metal.

She walked over to the sedan and knocked the designated three times on the window. A forty-something man opened the door and stood. Stubble formed a crown on his bald head.

"Let's make this quick," she said.

"In this line of business, you should take a moment to get to know your associates." His voice was calm, but that wasn't what disturbed her the most. A gun-toting militia nut would've made sense to her, but he was everything she didn't expect. Dressed in a navy suit with handkerchief, he looked like a stockbroker. What else hadn't she planned for?

"I'm not a cop," she said. "If that's what you mean."

He looked over her shoulder. "You were supposed to come alone."

"She's here for my safety." The rain picked up slightly, dotting his glasses, but he didn't take his eyes from her. Erika's dumpster comment began to freak her out. "Are we going to do this or not?"

"I take it you brought cash?" He opened a black umbrella.

If she answered truthfully, would he rob them? It wasn't as though they could go to the police. "I want to see the guns first."

"I see." He paused. "Well, we're not going to get anywhere unless somebody leaps." He walked back and opened the trunk. She couldn't shake her sinking feeling as she stared at the dozen handguns, neatly harnessed on gray felt.

She pulled out the money. "My friend snapped your license plate on the way in here. If anything happens to me—"

"Right, fine," he said. "Now what can I get you? Something for your purse?"

"If I have to shoot someone, I don't want them getting back up."

"Okay." He looked as though her answer surprised him. "Any of these will pack a punch. For your body size, you'll probably want a nine millimeter with Cop Killer or hollow point ammunition for maximum yield."

She'd emptied an entire clip into Jarod's head, and he'd still stolen her son. "Which ones do the most damage?"

"That depends." He opened a box and showed her bullets packed in foam. "Armor-piercing brass core can punch through metal. Small clean holes." That didn't sound like anything Jarod couldn't heal from. He held up a new box. "But Black Rhinos shatter into tiny razors on impact. They carry punch and even cut through Kevlar."

He handed her his umbrella. In two deft moves, he loaded the gun. It was over. He was going to shoot her right there. She almost ran, but at the last second, he turned and fired at an aluminum keg next to a cold campfire. The bullet ripped a massive hole and spun the keg. For seconds after, the hills rumbled.

"As you can see, not only does it deliver, but the sound wave can scare off potential attackers as well."

She took a second to quiet her beating heart, and then handed him back the umbrella. She'd seen enough. "How much for all the Rhino bullets you have and four handguns?"

"We need to talk," Erika said from behind. Damn. The gunfire must have scared her, but how had she walked up so quietly?

"Excuse us," Vivian said to him calmly, but inside she was panicking. They walked back to the Prius.

"I think he's okay," Vivian said. "But I need you to stay with the car."

"Just what do you think you're doing?"

"I'm getting my son back."

"Right." Erika crossed her arms. "With armor-piercing bullets."

"Please just trust me." She checked to make sure the man hadn't moved. For the time being, he seemed content to wait. "I know what I'm doing."

"You said those exact words when you dropped out of college to marry that jerk. And I told myself that it wasn't my place to push, but I won't sit back this time."

"You don't understand."

"Oh, I get it just fine," Erika said. "You're scared, and you're about to go off half-crazy."

Vivian wanted more than anything to just tell her. But Jarod's deformity and lightning storms? The radio in the room upstairs? It was too much. She wouldn't have believed it if she hadn't seen it.

"I have to get him back tonight," Vivian said.

"Cody is going to grow up without a mother. Do you want that?"

"Of course not." Her voice shook.

"Then help me. Why do you have to do things the hard way?"

"I'm not trying—"

"Better yet, you tell me why it's even smart to bring a gun. What if you killed somebody? What then?"

Despite the wind, Phil's screams echoed in her mind louder. "He murdered those boys in front of us."

"That's no excuse for you to become a murderer, too."

"Dammit. He's not human." The words slipped out.

"You should have thought of that before you married him."

"That's not what I mean." She paused, trying to think of a way out of this mess. Only the truth came to mind. Erika deserved at least that. "After he killed those kids last night, I shot him in the head. He stood back up and pulled Cody from my arms."

"Excuse me?" Erika gave her a look, and she knew that she'd just blown it. "Are you trying to say that he's not a human being?"

"I'm not sure what he is."

"I *knew* something was wrong with that man."

Wait. She couldn't have heard right. "You believe me?"

"Why didn't you tell me about this before?"

"And sound like a crazy person?"

Suddenly, Erika looked around as if realizing some truth. She turned and began speed walking over to the man. "Hey."

"What are you doing?" Vivian followed close behind. "I don't know about this guy."

Erika waved her away as they approached the sedan.

"Yes?" he said. The trunk lid was down, but it was still cracked.

"How much for all the guns you have in there?" Erika asked him.

"That's going to be pretty expensive. Are you sure you—"

"Yeah," Erika said. "And we want all of those exploding bullets, too." She motioned to the money in Vivian's hand with her eyes, so she handed it to him. "We're getting Cody back tonight."

Vivian nodded.

"Then that leaves only one more thing." The man closed the trunk, reached into his back pocket, and flashed a badge. "You have the right to remain silent. Anything you say or do can be used against you in a court of law."

16

Minutes passed like days in the cinderblock room. On the far side of the desk at which Vivian sat, a video camera rested on a tripod. A trail of wires led from it to a blank television screen. She dropped her head into her hands. For the last year and a half, some version of this moment had haunted her dreams. How could she have let it come to this?

A buzz preceded a loud click, and the steel door opened. Carrying a file in one hand and mug in the other, a giant officer, maybe six-five, entered the room. He looked as though he spent every waking moment lifting weights.

"Why am I still here?" Vivian asked.

"We'll get to that." He set his items down, rolled up his sleeves, and placed his badge face-up. The gun holstered under his arm seemed as menacing as he was. "I'm Detective Torres."

"It's been almost three hours." Did they know that she'd given them a phony ID and social? The license photos were nearly identical, and Erika had been prepped, but what if they ran her fingerprints? She needed to hurry this up before they realized that she wasn't Sarah Hoffman. "Please, I left my son with the babysitter."

"I'm sorry about that," he said. "This may take some time."

"How long?"

"That depends on you." He turned on the television.

Her face filled the screen. She wiped a smudge from her cheek, but it didn't help. Covered in a layer of sweaty grit, she looked guilty of any crime they wanted to throw at her.

"Where's Erika?" she asked.

"You two have been charged with possession of illegal weapons."

She relaxed slightly. If they'd matched her prints, the kidnapping charges would've come up.

"Before we start, would you like anything to drink?"

"Can we just get this over with?" She realized that she was biting her lower lip and stopped.

"I'm not sure that Russell Cotters would like that."

"Who?"

"Deputy Cotters." He walked back and sat across from her. "You know, the officer that we found strangled to death in your hospital bathroom this morning."

God no. They had her.

"I don't know what you're talking about," she said.

"Drop the act, Vivian. We know you're not Sarah Hoffman. You're only going to dig yourself deeper."

"He was dead when I woke up," she said.

"Then how did you get out of the cuffs?" He paused, but what could she tell him? That a psychopath named Stromsky who worked for the Carmichael family had murdered that officer? What about the boys that Jarod had killed last night? They were going to pin this on her.

All of it.

"Tell you what," Detective Torres said. "We'll get back to that one. When was the last time you talked to your sister Tamara?"

Tammy, that bitch. She'd obviously called the police last night. And probably didn't care that Vivian had almost died. Or that Cody had been taken.

"We haven't spoken in years," she said.

Torres leaned back in his chair. He drummed his fingers on the table. "If you insist on lying—"

"I haven't seen her."

"You just happened to be found unconscious a few blocks from her house this morning."

"I was on my way there," she said, "but I had an asthma attack."

"I'll be honest." Torres ran his fingers through his hair and finished by scratching behind his ear. "The chief thinks you look good for all of these." He reached into the folder and slapped down a crime scene photo of the dead cop from that morning.

She turned away.

"No, you look," he said. "Look."

One after the other. Jay-Jay on the garage floor. Phil in a pool of blood. Anthony's torso. He placed one final picture down gently.

"Oh God." She felt sick. The body was unrecognizable except for the heart tattoo on Tammy's mangled leg. "Is that…"

"What we could find of her. Most of the damage was caused by a neighbor's pit bull. The rest of the wounds appear to be inflicted by hooks of some kind."

"I didn't do it," she blurted.

"You were at all these crime scenes." He raised his voice.

The walls seemed to close in on her. She would never see her baby again.

"Please, you have to believe me," she said. "I couldn't do that."

"Personally, I find it hard to believe that you overpowered a two hundred pound officer this morning, but you'd better start explaining."

"I can't say anything."

Stromsky had made it clear. Any negative publicity for the Carmichaels would be a death sentence. But even if she stayed silent and went to jail, she wouldn't be able to protect her baby from that family.

"I'm the last friend you have here," Torres said. "But not for long. Any minute, my boss is going to come through that door. And there won't be much I can do for you after that."

"They'll kill my baby."

The door buzzed open. Erika stood outside in the hallway with two men on either side of her.

The one in the trench coat walked into the interrogation room. As soon as he looked up, Vivian's heart raced. David Rankin. She'd never forget the birthmark on the left side of his forehead. Or the way his eyes used to swarm her body when Jarod wasn't looking.

"Stop him," she shouted. "He's here to kill us."

"What the hell is going on?" Torres stood and towered over the room.

"This interview is over," Rankin said.

"Don't let him take us." She backed up against the far wall.

"Sit down." Torres pointed at her. "Nobody's going anywhere."

It was now or never. If she didn't trust somebody, Rankin would drive Erika and her to some deserted lot and shoot them.

"My husband murdered all those boys last night," she said. "Jarod Carmichael killed them all."

"Excuse me?" Torres asked.

"This witness has fled from federal protection," Rankin said loudly. "I've got all the documents here. She's due in court tomorrow." He pulled out several papers and handed them over. "She's not allowed to say any more."

"We'll see about this," Torres said.

"Listen to him, Hector." A jowl-faced man came into the interrogation room from the hallway. He motioned to the video camera. Rankin walked over and unhooked it.

"What are you doing here, Chief?" Torres asked. "It's almost midnight."

"The paper work checks out," the chief said. From the way he avoided eye contact, she knew he was part of it. "This case falls under federal jurisdiction."

They continued arguing, but their voices faded into background noise.

'*Your son is going to grow up without a mother.*' Erika's voice repeated in her head.

Vivian's chest felt tight. She tried to take deep breaths but wheezed instead. At that moment, she could only think of Cody, poking at a pill bug and laughing to tears when it rolled into a ball. He was so tiny. Innocent. Her heart felt like it would tear from her chest. She collapsed to the floor.

"Call an ambulance." Torres raced over to her. The minute he leaned over, she unbuttoned his holster strap and grabbed the gun. To her surprise, it pulled free. She held it to his chest.

"Everybody get in here." She stood. At first, they looked stunned. Then they reached for their guns. "Do it now or I'll kill him. I swear to God."

"She means it," Torres said.

"Put your guns on the table and get in the corner," she told Rankin and the police chief. They both did it. She moved behind Torres's tall body, held the gun to his lower back, and led him into the hallway.

"It's not too late to stop this," he said.

"Is this the part where you say that you can protect us?" Erika asked. Then she slammed the interrogation room door shut, locking Rankin and the police chief inside.

"I'm so sorry," Vivian said. "Those were Jarod's people. If you stay, they'll kill you."

"We'll deal with that later," Erika said. She turned to Torres. "Is there a rear exit?"

He pointed. They walked quickly down the hallway, and then down a flight of stairs. As they opened the door at the bottom, Vivian expected a battalion of SWAT teams with laser scopes pointed at her chest. Instead, the parking lot was nearly deserted. Something didn't feel right. That had been way too easy. Was it a trap? Even if it was, that only meant she needed to be careful. She had to get Cody back tonight.

"Give Erika your keys," Vivian said to Torres. He reached into his front pocket and handed them over. She pushed the car alarm button. Across the parking lot, a Honda beeped.

"They're going to assume that you murdered Deputy Cotters now," Torres said. "They will shoot to kill."

"*They* can get in line," Vivian said, a little shocked at her own detachment. She pushed him over to the car with Erika leading the way.

"I'm serious," he said.

"That's why you're coming with us."

If they left him behind, he would run back and inform the police, and therefore Jarod's men, which vehicle to track. Any extra seconds could mean the difference between life and death. Besides, with weapons possession, grand theft auto, kidnapping, and murder charges, one hostage wasn't going change outcome.

"Get in," she said to Torres. "You're driving."

14

Vivian clutched Torres's gun as they turned into the almond orchard bordering Jarod's estate. Cody was close now, but her situation had never been worse. Jarod, his family, and the police would all shoot her on sight. With her money confiscated, she had no means to run anymore.

There was only one way to save the people she loved. She had to get Cody to safety. Then she had to go back to kill Jarod, or her baby would never be safe. In the junkyard, she'd emptied a clip into that bastard's head, and it hadn't been enough to stop him. Could he even be killed? She had to find a way. Even if it meant her own life, too.

"It's not too late to end this." Torres's head nearly hit the Accord's roof as the pocked road grew bumpier. "Before somebody gets hurt."

"Just pull over there." She pointed to the orchard's irrigation mains.

The most dangerous part wouldn't be breaking in. Carrying Cody back through the trees at night was almost impossible, she knew from when they'd escaped before. Still, she couldn't risk getting any closer without security spotting the car.

"Those officers won't stay locked up for long." He parked. "Every squad car is probably headed here now."

He was right. What if they had been followed? Looking back, she found only a plume of dust, glowed red by the car's brake lights. In the backseat, Erika didn't take her eyes from the side window. Vivian wished she'd never involved her.

"Let me bring you both back in." His deep voice forced her attention back. "I'll make sure that you're safe."

"If we'd trusted you," she said. "We'd already be dead."

"You're wrong." He pointed at her, and suddenly the gun in her hand seemed inadequate for his size. "Nobody was going to hurt you."

"Maybe you were daydreaming when your chief tried to hand us over to my husband's people."

"I don't know the agent who came for you," he said. "But Chief Watts is a good man. There's no way he's taken anything from your husband."

"That's the problem with you cops. They give you badges and guns, but nobody bothers to check whether or not you have any brains."

"Vivian," Erika said from the backseat. "This isn't helping."

"Or morals." She couldn't resist the jab. Her nerves were frayed, and with the entire world bearing down on her, she wouldn't be lectured. Especially by a man who either refused or was too stupid to see the circus of lies around him. "Just get out," she said.

They exited the car. Maybe a quarter mile in the distance, Jarod's estate stood alone. It seemed to light the entire orchard. Looking up, she found that it was actually a full moon, peering ominously through a canopy of bare branches. Erika walked up beside her.

"I'm so sorry," Vivian said.

"Don't." Erika's breath fogged in the chilly air. "I knew what I was getting myself into. Now what are we going to do with him?"

"Where are your handcuffs?" she asked Torres.

"Back at the station."

She guessed that he was lying, but there wasn't time to search or argue. "Have it your way. Get in the trunk."

"I can't let you go in there." He stepped toward them.

"My son's being held by a madman," Vivian said. "I will shoot you."

"Not everyone is against you." The concerned look on his face made her feel guilty for pointing the gun at him. "If you're innocent, I can help."

"No you can't," she said.

He seemed sincere, but it didn't matter. Even with the best intentions, one good cop was no match for Jarod's corruption machine.

"My daughter's name is Alexis." He moved forward again. "Don't make her grow up without a father."

"I'm serious." She pushed the gun out, but he didn't stop. She felt a hand on her shoulder.

"Maybe we won't kill you," Erika said. "But keep walking, and you're going to need crutches."

Taking cue, Vivian pointed the gun at his knee and cocked it. "Get in the trunk now."

"Fine," he said. "It's your ass."

She didn't feel bad as he cramped himself into the trunk. He should've just told them where the handcuffs were. As Vivian gently closed the lid, brittle leaves crunched in the distance. Though she knew that it was probably wildlife or just the wind, she couldn't shake the feeling that intent eyes watched from somewhere in the dark. She hated the idea of leaving Erika alone out here, but she had no choice.

"Before I go in there—"

"What's this I?" Erika asked. "I'm coming with you."

"No, I need you here."

"You need me in there. What if somebody finds you?"

"The alarm will sound, and Jarod's security staff will lockdown the premises. You won't be able to help."

"It's not up for discussion," Erika said. "I'm coming with you."

"Please just let me finish." Her chest felt like a dam ready to burst. If she died without completing her task tonight, what would Jarod say? That she left and didn't look back? That she never cared? He was just that low. "If anything happens to me, I need you to get Cody and take care of him."

Erika turned her head and stared down the aisle of the trees. A brisk wind kicked up, dancing a swell of dead leaves around their feet. She realized *what* she had just asked. Yes, they were almost sisters, but the responsibility was too much. If Jarod were alive, how could she expect Erika to get him? The request was insane.

"I'm sorry," Vivian said. "It's too much."

"No." As Erika turned back, she wiped her eyes. Vivian realized that she hadn't been looking for a way out. "I swear on my life that I will get him."

"God, thank you." She hugged her.

"Please." Erika pulled away. "I'd never let the little man stay with that prick."

"If I'm not out in an hour," Vivian said. "Let Detective Torres out of the trunk, and you'll need to come for me."

"I will."

"No goodbyes," Vivian said.

Before Erika could protest, she turned and ran. Minutes later, she approached the clearing around the estate.

This was crazy. From here, the white stucco wall seemed taller. Maybe eight or nine feet, with new blaring lights running along the top like some secret government facility. Had he rebuilt it because she escaped that night? And if so, did he know about the small window in the corner of the wine cellar that wasn't attached to the security system? None of that mattered. Her baby needed her.

She tucked the gun in her jeans and sprinted forward. Somehow, she'd find a way inside.

18

Cody tried to sleep, but he didn't like this bedroom. He didn't like the Pikachu poster. Or Dora the Explorer stuffed animal. There were lots of toys, but none of them were his. When Mommy came to get him, he would tell her that he hated this room. Then they could go away and hide from Daddy again. He hoped she would get here soon.

A creaky noise behind him. He covered his head with the blanket. Hush quiet, he peeked out. There was Mister Vincent sitting on Horsey.

"Don't mind me." He rocked back and forth. "I'm just keeping watch. Making sure that nothing tries to come and get you tonight."

"Do you see Elmo?" Cody uncovered himself.

"You mean over there?" Mister Vincent nodded at the big Sesame Street painting on the wall.

"He looks at me."

"That's nothing to fuss about, but I'll keep an eye on him if it makes you feel better." Mister Vincent pointed to a door that was open just a little bit on the other side of the room. "That closet though, well, that's a whole different story. No telling what's hiding in there."

"Go check." He pulled up the blankets.

"It'll be fine as long as I'm here." He stopped rocking. "I know what will take your mind off all that. What do you say we play our game again?"

"No." He hated that game more than he hated all the toys. The game felt bad. It made Daddy mean last night. "I don't want to."

"I know how you feel, but I already told you it was an accident. Nothing much you can do about that. Let's just try it for a little while and see how it goes."

"No," he shouted. "I'm never going to do it again."

"If that's what you want, but I'll have to leave if you don't want to play. I just hope whatever's in that closet stays put."

The door looked like it moved.

"Don't go," Cody said. "Stay here."

"If you're not going to open the gateway for me, I have to leave."

He really didn't want to be alone now, but he couldn't do that again. Jay-Jay and Phil were nice. Cody felt sad. They were dead, and it was all his fault.

"I don't want to talk about the game anymore," Cody said.

"That's too bad for your Mommy. If the doorway was open, I might've been able to protect her tonight."

"Where is she? Is she hurt?"

"She's here now, but I wouldn't get too excited. Your mommy's going to die tonight."

"No," Cody yelled. "You're lying."

But Mister Vincent didn't lie about Jay-Jay. And Aunt Tammy. And Phil either. They were all dead. Mister Vincent never lied.

"Don't touch Mommy." He tried not to cry, but he couldn't stop. "Don't hurt her."

"It's not me you need to worry about, son."

Mister Vincent said something else, but Cody didn't want to hear him. He was so scared, and he was crying too loud. Mister Vincent tried to put his arm around him.

"Daddy, help," he screamed. Anyone help. He jumped off the bed and ran to the bedroom door. He had to find Mommy. He had to save her.

ひつひつ

Jarod sat in the study's quiet darkness, holding his Glock to the side of his face. He pulled the trigger. The clack of the empty chamber vibrated his skull, soothing him. Vivian had been stupid to get herself arrested. Clack.

How she'd managed to elude him for more than a year was a fucking mystery. And now, the situation was even more complicated. Police were involved and God knows who else. Clack. Still, it would be fine. Rankin would take care of it. He'd be back at the estate with her soon. Jarod couldn't wait to shoot her in the heart.

A muffled cry came from the hallway. With his good hand, he fumbled to load the clip. He stood, crept across the cold marble, and pushed the intercom. "What was that?"

Only static came back. Rankin had doubled the security shifts. Where was his staff? Quietly, he opened the door. The deep splash of running water echoed down from the second story balcony.

"It was an accident," Cody shouted. What was he doing out of his bedroom? "I didn't mean to let him in."

Jarod raced down the hallway and up the stairs. At the top, the bathroom was locked. He shouldered the door twice, and it splintered open.

He raised the gun and charged in. What the hell was going on? This wasn't the right room. It wasn't even the estate anymore. Directly in front of him, lit only by two candelabra, a man in all black knelt next to a claw-footed Victorian bathtub. His sleeves were rolled up.

The hairs raised on Jarod's neck. Standing beside the man, he recognized himself wearing only boxers. He couldn't have been more than seven years old. But if that were true, then that meant…He remembered little of his biological father, except those bloodshot eyes.

"It won't happen again," his younger self said through tears. Had he ever been so weak? No. None of this was real. He must've fallen asleep in the study.

"Pray for forgiveness." His father grabbed a gallon of bleach.

"I didn't mean to let him in."

"And you'd better pray it stays sealed." Icy water brimmed the tub's edge, but he continued pouring until the jug emptied. The torn plastic wrap of several twenty-pound ice bags sat at his feet. He turned off the faucet.

"It won't happen again," his younger self cried.

"You're right it won't." Spittle shot from his father's lips as he shoved the boy into the water. A flood burst over the side.

"Mister Vincent." The boy managed to push his head above the waterline. "Help me."

"Get away from him," Jarod shouted.

Looking up to the ceiling, his father said, "Forgive me for what I brought into this world."

"You son of a bitch." Jarod raised his gun.

"Forgive me for what I now have to do." The old man pushed down harder. The thrashing became violent.

Jarod pulled the trigger repeatedly. Thunder roared through the bathroom. He waited for screaming. He longed for blood, but the man remained untouched.

"Can't change what can't be changed," a raspy voice said from behind, and everything paused. Splashing fans of bleach water were suspended in midair. Candle flames whooshed every direction. His father sat frozen in time, holding him under. Jarod spun to find Vincent standing in the doorway. In the dim light, his facial skin looked antiqued, his teeth gritty.

"What is this?" he demanded. "Why have you brought me here?"

"You weren't right again after that night." The look of pity on Vincent's face made Jarod furious. "It's time you knew everything. They're coming again—"

"Get out of my head now." He slammed the old man against the door and shoved the gun underneath his chin. "You think I forgot about your mind games earlier."

"That was just a warning to keep you thinking straight."

"I don't know what you are, but I'd better never see you again."

"You're making a big mistake."

"Are you threatening me?" Jarod moved the gun from his chin to his forehead.

"The sooner you figure out that I'm not the enemy, the better off you're going to be."

Jarod motioned to himself in the bathtub, trapped under the torrent water. "Is this your idea of better off?"

"You don't know the half of what I've done for you." Vincent's calm tone sent chills through his body. For a split second, the old man's pupils seemed unnaturally large. "What do you think you're going to do with that gun anyway?"

He was right. Jarod released him. As he stepped back, droplets of water bounced off his body and slowed to new suspended positions.

"None of this is real," he said.

"Unless you convince that boy of yours to listen to me, you're going to find out just how real this is."

"I won't tell you again," Jarod said. "Stay away from me and my son."

"You'd better clean out your ears." Vincent pointed at him. "You think you're clever, waiting for Vivian to fly into your trap, but Mr. Kevin Stromsky is outside your house right now."

"What?" There was no way. Stromsky had one purpose in life, and he only worked for the Carmichael family. "My mother would never send that man here. To my house."

"Oh come now," Vincent said. "If you insist on being a fool, then maybe—"

"She wouldn't dare."

"She's afraid of what you are, son."

"And what's that?" Jarod asked.

"The mouth of God."

It wasn't just ridiculous. It was obscene. He pointed to his zealot of a father, posed like a wax figure. "You mean this God?"

"Don't get trapped with words," Vincent said. "It just means that you've got the sight. Like your son, you see and know things you shouldn't. It's been in your family for generations. It has made the Carmichaels a wealthy clan."

"I built this empire," Jarod said. "Not some psychic bullshit, and I haven't even seen you before today."

"The gift is fragile." Vincent seemed sad as he looked over at the bathtub. "After your father did this, your gift was broken. Couldn't see me anymore. Last night, that changed when your son opened the gates for me."

"I can't remember last night."

"Let me show you." The old man reached over, and Jarod flinched. "I will show you why your mother sent Mr. Kevin Stromsky."

Slowly, Jarod held out his hand. As Vincent grabbed his wrist, images of snapping bone and tearing flesh filled him. A bald kid pleaded for his life. Jarod dug claws into his soft neck. He yanked his arm away.

"It's a lie." He backed up. "None of this is real."

Vincent looked annoyed. "I don't lie."

"Get the fuck out of my head," Jarod said.

"Maybe you need to see the rest of what happened that night."

Right then, the suspended water splashed down.

"I'm dreaming." Jarod turned just as his father bared his teeth and pushed down with both arms. "This is just a dream."

The struggle became frenzied, until the small arm over the side of the tub stopped moving. Suddenly, a hole exploded in his father's forehead. Blood sprayed against the back wall.

A gloved man walked in, holding a silenced gun. Only after a second, did Jarod realize who it was. His hair hadn't grayed yet, and he was thirty years younger, but there was no mistaking those soulless blue eyes. Stromsky walked over and pulled Jarod's limp body from the tub. His younger self coughed water, and began breathing.

Stromsky then moved to the bathroom's wall phone, picked it up, and dialed a number.

"Charlotte, my dear," he said in a pleasant voice. "It's finished." He paused. "Your son will be just fine with some rest. Maybe a spot of tea to warm him up. Shall I bring him over?"

"You've been warned," Mister Vincent said. "Do what you will."

And then Jarod was standing alone in his own bathroom. The porcelain sink was shattered, and several bullet holes had been punched in the tile. It wasn't real. It couldn't be, but what if Vincent was telling the truth?

"Sir," a voice called out. Heavy footsteps clomped up the stairs. Leon ran into the doorway and felt all over Jarod's body. "Are you hit?"

Had his whole life been a lie? Had his mother murdered his father? She couldn't have. Could she? If she had her own husband killed, Jarod wasn't safe.

"Sir," Leon said louder. "Mr. Carmichael."

"My son," Jarod said. "Get him. We're leaving."

"Where to?"

"Just get him. We'll decide on the way."

19

Vivian ducked behind the hedges that bordered the estate's kitchen. At ground level, she found the basement window that she'd escaped from before. Grabbing onto a water faucet for support, she kicked the window twice and shattered it. The remaining glass shards broke off as she squeezed through feet first and dropped into the dank cellar. No alarm sounded. In fact, there was no movement anywhere.

This was all wrong. When they'd escaped before, the security staff had nearly seen them several times. And Jarod had been caught off guard that night. This had to be a trap, but it didn't matter. It only meant that she needed to be smart. Jarod had always underestimated her. Hopefully he'd do the same tonight.

A sliver of moonlight shined on the rows of temperature-controlled wine racks. Navigating the dark maze by touch, she reached the staircase that led to the kitchen above. Something crunched behind her. She spun around but could barely see. There it was again, louder now. Back where she'd entered.

"Mommy." A whisper echoed through the dark cellar.

She almost ran back but stopped. The voice had been so quiet that it could have been anyone. Or anything. But what if it was Cody? Jarod's security guards wouldn't lurk.

"Where are you, baby?" she called out softly and took a step to the side. If it wasn't him, she didn't want them to know her position.

"In the dark." The hushed voice sounded more like Cody this time.

Please let it be him. If it was, they were less than five minutes from safety. From here, they could even make it to the Mexican border before sunrise. She almost ran forward but caught herself. Hope was a dangerous emotion. In the past, it had led her to take risks. It had led her into Jarod's arms. Never again. Tonight, she couldn't slip up.

"Step into the light so I can find you." She moved back to the edge of the aisle, but she didn't dare aim her gun.

Peeking around the corner, she gasped. Cody stood in a spattering of broken glass and soil. He wore a footed pajama suit that she'd never seen before.

"Oh baby." She raced over to him and dropped to her knees.

"Don't leave me here," he said with his arms crossed over his chest.

"Never ever." She tucked the gun into her jeans and moved him from the broken glass. "Are you hurt?"

"I bumped my head." Dried tears streaked his dirty face. How long had he been in the basement? That fucker. If she ever got Jarod alone, he wouldn't walk away this time.

Carefully, she moved a ringlet of hair away from the cut on the side of Cody's forehead. In the phosphorescent moonlight, the wound appeared dark purple. Was it infected? She couldn't tell. What if he had a concussion? They needed to get to a doctor.

"Are you alone?" She tried to sound calm, but her voice shook with rage. "Did your father lock you down here?"

"He doesn't know." He put his hands on her cheeks. "I don't want you to die."

"I'm here now, baby. I swear no one will *ever* take you away from me again." She squeezed him close and wished for more time. Just a few seconds to hold him, but they had to get to safety. "Everything's going to be okay. We're just going to crawl outside."

"No." He stared up at the window. Had he heard something? She listened, but only wind howled through the broken pane.

"It's okay. We've done this before." She tried to pick him up, but he jumped back.

"What's wrong?" she asked.

"Not that way." He shook his head. "Not that way."

Did he remember the first time they ran? For several seconds, she'd put him above by himself. Though it had been a warm night, she'd thought that he'd never stop shivering.

"You have to calm down," she said.

"We need Daddy."

"What?" she asked. He looked at the ground. There wasn't time for his confusion. She picked him up. "We've got to go."

"Not without Daddy." He pushed away from her chest.

"Baby, please. You have to be quiet."

"He's out there."

She ducked into a shadowy walkway. Wine racks raised to the ceiling on both sides of them. They were concealed in darkness, but the window was still in view.

"Who's waiting?" she whispered. "Is your father outside?"

"Not that way." He clamped his arms around her neck.

What were they going to do? Any other exit from the house would sound the alarm. But had Cody really seen someone? He'd been hiding down here. Probably all night. She needed to find out if he actually knew something.

"Baby," she said. "Tell me who's outside."

"The bad man."

"Did you see him?" she whispered. "What does he look like?" In the darkness, she couldn't tell if he understood the question, but he didn't answer her. "What color is his hair?"

"White," he whispered.

Oh God. Stromsky was waiting outside for them. But why? The basement seemed to grow colder as she realized the truth. The Carmichaels had never planned to let her raise Cody. They wanted her dead. Or to set her up. Well, whatever twisted plans they had for her, it wasn't going to work.

A flashlight shined through the window. The beam shimmied closer. She heard voices over the wind.

"We have a break-in," a man's voice said.

"Call it in," somebody else answered. "She's inside the house."

They were trapped. In seconds, the entire estate would be swarming with security. No matter what, they couldn't stay here. She picked up Cody and pressed his head against her shoulder. There was only one option. The mansion was huge, with hundreds of hiding places. Hopefully, Jarod would think she'd already escaped. Somehow, she'd have to get word to Erika. One problem at a time.

Something slammed against the wall outside. The guard must have dropped flat on his stomach, because his face filled the tiny window. Did he notice them? At least he didn't shine the light in her direction. Then she saw the bullet hole in his forehead. She clamped her hand over her mouth. Slowly, his face was dragged from view.

"If we don't find Daddy," Cody said. "Mister Vincent said you'll die."

Stromsky really had been right outside the entire time. Waiting, just as Cody had said. She couldn't hide from the truth anymore. Cody had warned her because he knew what would happen if they'd climbed through that window. The same way that he'd known to wait for her in the basement. The same way he'd known Jay-Jay's name last night.

All day, she'd silenced the voice in her head that told her Cody was somehow connected to everything. The storm in the warehouse. Maybe even Jarod's transformation. Did that mean…No. Never. Genetics or not, they weren't the same person. Her baby was not destined to become that monster. As Vivian reached the staircase, she was certain they'd be dead if she hadn't listened to him.

'If we don't find Daddy, Mister Vincent said you'll die.'

"I'm so sorry I didn't believe you," she whispered, and then started up the steps. "Now let's go get your father."

She prayed that Jarod was in human form.

20

Vivian stood in complete darkness on the last step of the basement's staircase. Through the walls, a churning dishwasher masked all other sounds. She cracked open the door. Light from the estate's central courtyard striped the deserted kitchen. She moved to the counter and set Cody down.

Where could she hide him when dealing with Jarod? Obviously not in the basement. Or under the kitchen sink with the chemicals. Every closet seemed inadequate.

"You have to be fucking kidding me." Jarod walked into the connected hallway. She grabbed Cody, ducked, and held her finger over her lips to tell him to be quiet.

"The police picked her up with almost fifty thousand in cash," someone else answered. She peeked around the countertop. David Rankin stood in the doorway. If he'd already escaped the interrogation room and made it here, the police wouldn't be far behind. "She was busted trying to buy guns from an undercover."

"If you were doing your job, none of this would be happening," Jarod said. Though he was out of view, his voice sounded human. "You should've found her last year. Now she magically escapes from a goddamn police precinct."

"It was beyond my control. I had the police chief send most of his staff home. How could I know that she'd steal some idiot local's gun and escape?"

"Please give me one more excuse. It'll be your last."

"Sir," a third voice echoed down from what sounded like the upstairs balcony. "Your son isn't in his room."

Where could they hide? The estate would be crawling with security soon. Jarod grabbed Rankin and slammed him against the front door. As they argued, Vivian carried Cody down the hallway.

They'd already searched his room. It might buy some time to go there. She ran to the rear of the house, up the back staircase, and into the third door on the left. Leaving the lights off, she tiptoed through a mess of toys.

"I want you hide under here." She set him down next to his bed. He crawled backwards until only his head poked out. "No matter what happens, stay hidden until I come back."

As she kissed his forehead, she expected him to resist, but he slinked underneath. Did that mean she was making the correct choice? How much did he actually know with his sixth sense? Not enough, probably, or he would've warned her that Jarod was going to show up at the cabin last night. Wouldn't he have?

The hardwood floor squeaked behind her. Was somebody there? She didn't dare look. The bedroom light clicked on. Giant stuffed animals and plastic robots overpopulated the bright yellow room.

"I told you what would happen if you ever left me," Jarod said. His footsteps moved closer.

"We need to talk." With the gun tucked into the front of her jeans, she couldn't turn around or he'd see it.

"Didn't I warn you?"

"There are bigger problems than us here," she said.

"And like the whore that you are, you just had to test me."

"Don't you dare." In all of her life, she'd never felt so low. With her baby hiding underneath his bed, witnessing her worst mistake. His own father. "Stromsky is outside."

"I know." He pulled her hair away from her ear, and her skin crawled.

"He's already killed two of your guards."

"That's why I'm going to ask you only once." He smelled rancid, as if he hadn't bothered to shower off the blood of his victims. "Where's my son, Vivian?"

He hadn't been watching long enough to know that Cody was under the bed.

"You stole him from me." She tried to sound desperate. "What have you done with my baby?"

"I stole him from *you*?" His words were quiet. "My own son."

"I'm his mother. He needs to be with me—"

He yanked her hair and flung her. Sharp pain punched her thigh as she crashed over the dresser. She dropped to her hands, trying to conceal the gun as she pulled it from her waistband.

"You were nothing before me," he shouted. "I made you. And you run off with my son in the middle of the night without even leaving a fucking note."

"Listen to me." She coughed. Pain stabbed the left side of her chest. "Please, you have to listen. Stromsky came to see me in the hospital today. He wants you dead."

"For the first week, I thought my wife and son had been kidnapped. Do you have any fucking clue of what that feels like?"

"I'm sorry." For that, she truly meant it. Nobody should have to endure what she'd felt with Cody gone.

"Was he worth it?"

"What are you talking about?" she asked.

"The bastard you left me for. The one you've been fucking all this time."

"There was no one." She finally looked up into his psychotic eyes.

What was she thinking? It was crazy to think that she could reason with this lunatic. And that arm. He'd lost it because of her. In her rush to get Cody, she hadn't even considered it. Even in human form, Jarod would never rest until she was dead now.

"I know you're not smart enough to hide from me all this time without help," he said. "So who is he?"

"Go to hell."

In a blur, he raced at her. She grabbed a fire truck from the ground and threw it at his face. As he blocked it, she jumped up and smashed the gun into his nose. He recoiled. A stream of blood poured down his face. She pressed the barrel against his forehead.

"You sick..." She stopped herself. Cody had warned her that they needed him. No, he had to be mistaken. Trying to reason with Jarod had nearly cost her life right now. If she didn't handle him now, she wouldn't get another chance. "You're never going to hurt us again."

"Mommy," Cody cried.

"Stay there." She glanced to make sure that he was still under the bed. He was. She looked back just as Jarod pulled his own gun. He pointed it at her chest. They stood arm to arm.

"Looks like we're going to die together," he said.

The bedroom door swung open. Just over Jarod's shoulder, Rankin aimed at her, too. Could this get any worse? She couldn't possibly shoot them both.

"Please," she said. What could she do? It was over. No, her only chance was to play on Jarod's jealousy. "I don't want to do this anymore. I've already lost everything."

"You should have thought of that before you ran out on me," Jarod said.

"You wanted to know who I was with all this time. It was David Rankin."

"What?" Rankin said from behind.

"I should have never run," she said quietly. If this was going to work, Jarod had to believe the lie. She lowered her gun and set it on the bed. "He convinced me to leave you. I wish I never would have. I know it's probably too late, but I just want to come back to you."

"She's lying," Rankin said.

"I couldn't have hidden from you all this time without his help. A few times, I tried to leave, but he said that you'd never take me back."

"That's crazy," Rankin shouted. "She's yours. I wouldn't touch her."

"You think I haven't seen the way you two used to look at each other." Jarod spun around and fired. Two neat holes punched in Rankin's throat. The momentum of the bullets carried him over the balcony's railing.

Vivian snatched the gun from the bed and fired. Cody screamed something, but gunfire drowned him out as she fired again. Blood sprayed over a mural of Big Bird's face. Slamming into the wall, Jarod stained a crimson trail down the paint. He slumped to the ground. She ran over to him and grabbed his gun.

"You'd better kill me." He clutched his hand over the bloody hole in his chest.

"No." Cody raced over and held her leg.

She kept her gun pointed as she knelt. "Go back underneath the bed."

"No," he cried.

"Now."

"Mister Vincent said stop," Cody shouted.

Jarod began laughing. Then harder as everything went dark. Stromsky must've cut the power. After a second, her eyes adjusted to the moonlight through the window.

"You'd better listen to the boy," Jarod said. "You don't want to make old Vincent mad at you."

Security would be here any second. The police, too. And Stromsky was outside waiting. She had to kill Jarod before it was too late. This might be her only chance. She pushed Cody back and raised the gun.

"No. We need Daddy." Cody's voice trembled. He began crying. Tears filled her eyes too as she held him back. "Don't hurt Daddy. Don't hurt Daddy."

"Stay back." She had to take control of the situation.

He pulled at her jeans in a violent tantrum.

"Mister Vincent said don't hurt Daddy," Cody screamed. "Or you'll die like the others."

21

Or you'll die like the others...' Cody's words repeated in Vivian's mind. She didn't know what to do. Listening to him had saved her life in the cellar. And it had nearly gotten her killed not five minutes later. Who was Mister Vincent? What did he want with her son?

Jarod still sat slumped against the wall. More than anything, she wanted to end this. Though she might never get another opportunity, after what she'd seen last night, she couldn't afford to take chances with things she didn't understand. For now, Jarod would live.

Cody tugged at her pant leg.

"Not now." She moved to the bedroom window and peeked out of the curtains. Although power to the estate had been shut off, the security lights lining the wall must have been on a separate breaker. They still illuminated the almond orchard. She checked her watch. In less than thirty minutes, Erika would let Torres out of the truck.

"Come on." She kneeled down to Cody. "We're leaving."

"With Daddy?"

"Your father will be fine." She ran her fingers through his hair and picked him up.

"You still don't get it." Jarod coughed and clutched the bullet wound in his shoulder. Even in the dark, she could see blood pooling on the floor under his elbow. "You won't make it down the driveway."

"Maybe," she said. "It looks clear now."

"Do you think the fly ever sees the spider's web?" Jarod asked.

"I won't stay and give you another opportunity to kill me."

"Don't worry. It'll come."

She moved over to him, pointed the gun just inches from his face, and said, "Just give me a reason."

"No." Cody shook his head.

Jarod let go of his wound and grabbed the gun's barrel with a wet hand. Gently, he moved it to his forehead. She could feel the end of her nightmare. Just pull the trigger and they could slip away, but she couldn't. Not unless she wanted to piss off Mister Vincent. With everything that had happened in the last few days, she couldn't risk it.

"What are you waiting for?" He smiled.

"Lie down and wait for Stromsky for all I care," she said. "Cody and I are going to live."

"You're already dead."

Vivian was disgusted that she'd ever loved him. "You're not even a man."

"For once you're right. I am the spider." His deep voice was monotone as he stared at the window. "No…I was the spider. Alone, watching the butterfly dance."

His ranting sounded like the previous night when he'd been that thing. Did that mean he would change soon? Screw it. Let Stromsky come in here and clean this mess. They were leaving him behind.

Both Jarod and Cody turned their heads in unison towards the corner of the bedroom. Nothing was there, except a spattering of toys. Their plastic smiles seemed malicious in the dim moonlight.

"Mister Vincent." Cody sounded relieved.

"There you are," Jarod said angrily.

Don't let this be happening. Don't let them be the same. But they were. Worse than that, if they could both see Mister Vincent, then there was no doubt. He did exist.

"Don't talk to him, baby," Vivian said.

"Fuck off." Jarod appeared to be talking to himself. He waited, and then said, "I hope she does die."

"What's going on?" she demanded.

"The safe," Cody whispered in her ear.

"What safe?" she asked Jarod. "What's in there? A weapon?"

He glared at her and then at Cody. Turning back, he said to Mister Vincent, "If he even is my son."

"You prick," she said.

"The safe," Cody repeated.

"There isn't one," she told him. "Do you mean the panic room?"

He looked to the corner, appeared to get confirmation, and nodded at her.

"We'll be trapped with him," she said. "Never."

"I'd listen to the man." Jarod seemed to get pleasure from her fear.

"Mommy, it's okay."

"Don't you talk to him," she told Cody and stepped away from the corner. "I don't know what you are. Stay away from my son. We're leaving."

"You're not going anywhere," Jarod said with a twisted grin. He held his bloody forefinger to his lips. Then he motioned at the door and whispered, "Vincent says we have a visitor just outside."

"We need to be quiet," she whispered in Cody's ear.

"In here," Jarod shouted.

The door slammed open. A flashlight beamed down first, and then swung up to her eyes.

"Drop the weapon." A voice boomed from the blinding light. "Now."

She shoved Cody back towards the toy box and aimed at Jarod. It wasn't Stromsky. She would've recognized the accent. He had to be one of Jarod's.

"Don't try to stop us," she said. "We're leaving."

"I don't want to hurt you, Vivian." He sounded familiar.

"Leon?" Please let it be him. The only friendly face on Jarod's security staff. "Is that you?"

"You know I can't let you hurt Mr. Carmichael."

"She shot me," Jarod hissed. "Kill her."

"Hold on," Leon said. "You're not paying me enough to murder anyone."

"Consider your salary tripled."

"You gonna buy me a suite in hell too?" He closed the door behind him. "Sorry boss, you can fire me tomorrow. Until then, my job is to keep you breathing. That's it."

"You will regret this," Jarod said.

"I *will* leave you behind if you don't watch it."

"Please, whatever is going on here has nothing to do with us." She lowered her gun, and he did the same. "I just want my baby back."

"If you let that bitch take my son—"

"Shut up. Both of you." Leon lowered the beam. With his hawkish eyes and pointed nose, he seemed determined. "There were eight men on duty tonight. None of them are answering their radios. The landlines are dead. My cell, too, which means that somebody's running a jammer."

"So do your fucking job and take care of her." Jarod pushed himself onto his feet, using the wall against his back.

"Right," Leon said sarcastically. "Mrs. Carmichael disabled seven members of the security detail. You both better listen. Whoever is doing this is damn good, so drop your bullshit if you want to live."

"The safe room," Jarod said. "Take me there."

"No." Vivian stepped back. "We'll be trapped."

"She's right," Leon said. "We shouldn't box ourselves in."

Jarod coughed violently this time, and she thought she saw blood on his teeth. Good.

"I need the first aid kit," Jarod said.

Leon seemed to consider it. "The landline in the safe room is hardwired into the system. It should still work. I could call in more men. The police."

Vivian motioned the gun at Jarod. "He'll kill me the second he gets the chance."

"Nobody's going to kill anyone," Leon said. "Isn't that right, sir?"

"It doesn't matter." Jarod turned to her. "Sooner or later, I will find you."

"I said isn't that right, Mr. Carmichael?" Leon shined the flashlight directly at him.

"Get that fucking thing off me."

"He's not going to do anything sinful." Leon moved the beam back to the floor. "Because he knows that me and Jesus go way back."

"I'm not paying you to—"

"And he also knows that me and Jesus used to fuck people up. Men much more powerful than he is, so we're not afraid."

Jarod didn't respond.

"I only want Cody safe," she said.

"I'll walk you out of here personally," Leon said. "But we have to go before it's too late."

Here it was. Alone, she was as good as dead. At least in the panic room, she could call Erika and warn her. Leon was a good man. He'd driven them to the hospital the night that Jarod had hurt Cody. And he'd stayed long after his shift had ended.

"Fine," she said. "But Cody stays with me."

"We have to go dark." He clicked off the flashlight. Her eyes adjusted after a second. Leon turned around and gently opened the door. After peeking outside, he whispered, "Move calmly. Do not stop until we reach the library."

Vivian held her breath as they walked into the darkened hallway. Leon was crouched in front, followed by Jarod, whose breathing sounded wet. Behind, she carried Cody.

Just before they turned the corner that led to the staircase, Jarod looked back and whispered, "Soon."

22

Erika blew warm breath into her hands. Her sneakers sank into soft dirt as she paced beside Detective Torres's car. Thirty-seven minutes. Viv should've been out by now. Or at least signaled for help.

All around, bare branches clacked together in the brisk wind. She listened for anyone trying to sneak up on her, but the dark orchard rustled in every direction. Nana Clara's Hoodoo BS embarrassed her to no end, but what she wouldn't give for one of those nasty rooster claws now.

A thumping startled her. Detective Torres started pounding the inside of the trunk again.

"Let me out of here." His shout was muffled. "I can't breathe."

Nobody should be boxed up like that. But once she set him free, would he help them? More likely, he'd drive them back to the police, who in turn would ship them back here.

To Vivian's shithead ex. Still, it had almost been an hour now, and no word.

"When I open this," she said. "Are you gonna help us?"

"Just let me out."

"I asked you a question. Are you going to hurt me?"

"Yes," he shouted. "I mean no."

From the panic in his voice, he sounded claustrophobic. Would he suffocate? No way the trunk was airtight. It was smarter to leave him be until it was time to go after Viv. But what if she was hurt? With no way to call for help. She looked at her watch. Forty-one minutes. What was she thinking letting that woman go off alone? This had gone too far.

She popped open the trunk. Looking in, she saw Torres fill the space to capacity. It took him a minute to work himself out. When he finally stood, he towered over her with shaking muscles. Maybe it had been worse in there than she had thought.

He grabbed her shoulders, spun her around, and slammed her chest into the driver's door.

"Take it easy," she said. "I could have left you in there."

"You've already been read your rights." He pinned her wrists behind her back with one giant hand and frisked her with the other. "Where's Vivian?"

"She went in for her son," Erika said over her shoulder. "We've got to help her."

"Help her?" he said. "Do you have any idea of what kind of trouble she's in? The trouble you're in? Kidnapping is a felony. Mandatory prison time."

"Do you think she gives a damn about what you're going to do to her if she makes it out with her son alive?"

"Save it," he said. "If her husband was such a danger, she should have come to us sooner."

"Really? I wonder why we never thought of that."

"I know that this is hard for you to believe." He turned her around and held her against the car. "But the police department doesn't sit around cooking up conspiracies against rich housewives and their friends."

"Housewives?" The nerve of this jerk. "USC Medical. You probably missed it while attending your community college. It's the one with the stadium."

"All that schooling to become an armed felon," he said. "Money well spent."

"If you cops would do your jobs for once, then maybe we wouldn't have to do it for you." She caught herself. Running her mouth wasn't going to help.

"Believe me," he said. "Nobody in my precinct even knows who you are."

"Right. Government agents scoop up all your suspects in the middle of the night."

"If we're so corrupt," he said. "Then why do you need my help?"

"Because I think that you're on the level," she told him. "What if you don't know everything? What if we're not lying?"

"That's not my job to figure out." Leaning into the car, he retrieved his cell phone. "If you're innocent, the courts will clear you."

"Call your boss, and we'll be dead in an hour."

"That man saved my life a hundred times." With his breath puffing in the air, he looked like a bull. After pausing a second, he said calmly, "We follow procedure for a reason."

"Please don't make that call," Erika said. "Just check out the house first."

He dialed the phone and waited. "Chief Watson."

Their plan had failed. This asshole was too dumb to pay attention to anything but his precious rules. At the next opportunity, she needed to get inside to warn Vivian.

"Stay put." He walked two steps and dialed again. He took another step.

Erika darted toward the lights in the distance. He yanked her turtleneck. She leaned forward and tumbled into a dirt cloud. He fell to his hands and knees, too.

She sprinted forward. Within minutes, she reached a clearing in the trees. Security lights on the outer wall of Jarod's estate blinded her. Looking back, she didn't see Torres anywhere. She ducked down and moved silently along the tree line. Before going in, she needed more distance between them.

Something crunched to her left.

"What is our status?" a voice said quietly. Erika hid behind a tree trunk.

"Waiting for confirmation," someone else answered.

Had the cops already arrived? No, they wouldn't be driving that child kidnap van. Shadows merged together, but even from here she could see at least three men dressed completely in black.

One silhouette broke from the rest. He pointed to where she'd just come from. Maybe a hundred yards back, Torres lumbered into the lights of the clearing. Someone must have been watching over her tonight, because none of these men seemed to notice her. And they were less than forty feet away. One of them aimed an assault rifle at Torres.

"Let him go," the first voice said. "Twenty minutes. We'll catch him in the sweep."

All four men moved to the far side of the van. If they weren't police, then who were they? No one to screw with, she guessed. Sneaking backwards, she deliberately avoided crunching any leaves until the van was out of sight.

Twenty minutes to find Vivian and Cody. Then, armed men would storm that house. By then, she and Vivian needed to be long gone.

"I hope you're watching out for the good guys." She kissed her necklace crucifix, raced into the clearing, and climbed over the wall.

23

The hallway stretched before Vivian, cool and dark as a train tunnel. Keeping one hand on the wall for guidance, she tried to keep a safe distance from Jarod, whose stench grew more rotten by the second.

Blindly, they inched forward, until reaching the balcony. Above, stars through the skylight gave the estate a twilight glow. Leon crouched at the top of the staircase. He held up his palm to say *stop*.

"Don't make a sound," he whispered. "I'm going down to check if it's safe."

"If you leave us here—" Jarod took several short breaths. "I will find you."

"Of course you will." Leon turned and moved silently downstairs.

Cody wrapped his arms around her neck so tightly, that she had trouble breathing.

"We're almost there," she whispered in his ear.

Still clutching his arm to his chest, Jarod leaned against the wall for support. He closed his eyes. Could one bullet in his shoulder have done so much damage? She hoped so. Leon reappeared at the foot of the stairs and waved them forward.

Halfway down, Jarod began staggering. She desperately tried to hold him up. As he tumbled, the stairway shook, finishing with a sickening thud as his head smacked the marble floor.

"Move," Leon whisper shouted. He put Jarod's arm over his shoulder, and she ran downstairs. Blood, black as motor oil in the dark, dripped from a gash in his forehead.

"He's coming." Cody gripped her hair and pulled it.

They ran to the double oak doors of the library. As Vivian walked inside, she held one arm forward to avoid bumping into anything. Leon shut the doors behind her.

"Mommy."

"It's okay, baby." She kissed his cheek. "We'll be safe soon."

Leon clicked on his flashlight and handed it to her. The thin beam barely held back the darkness. He locked the doors to the library.

"He's here," Cody said.

"Where?" She shined the light around the library. "Where is he, baby?"

He pointed to the doors from which they'd just come.

"Open the panels to the safe room." Leon began dragging Jarod under his arms. "I'll meet you there."

"The power is off."

"It has its own backup battery," he said. "Hurry."

A rattle came from the door, and something flicked her face. Shining the beam over, she saw wood chips flitter to the ground. Another bullet hole punched through the door handle. Stromsky was right outside.

"Move now," Leon shouted.

The light beam bounced erratically as she raced behind the center bookshelf. Feeling under Jarod's desk, she pushed the switch. Twenty feet away, mechanized wall panels pushed outwards and slid to the side. Leon set Jarod down and keyed in the code. A piston released the inner vault doors.

Gunshots forced her to the ground. She smothered Cody underneath her. Glancing up, she saw Leon drag Jarod by his shirt, backing up as he fired his gun.

"Kill that light," he shouted.

She clicked it off. Muzzle flashes strobed his body in the darkness. He took cover in the niche created by the safe room doors.

"Get in here," he said to her.

As she stood, bullets cracked into the wood next to her head. She jumped back and shouted, "I can't."

"I'll cover you."

For a brief moment, the gunfire lulled. Metal clicks echoed in the darkness. More shots and the smell of burning powder. She smothered Cody with her arms and raced into the infrared glow of the panic room. Seconds later, Leon followed her in dragging Jarod. The doors wheezed shut.

"Is that it?" She struggled to catch her breath. In the reddish lights, the place looked like a government bomb shelter. "Can he get inside?"

"This room is only a deterrent." Leon flipped three switches on the center console. A subsonic hum, barely audible, pulsed the air. Several overhead panel lights powered on. "It will buy us time."

"How much?"

"No way to know," he said.

Leon dragged Jarod to the center of the structure. Vivian almost felt secure inside these polished gunmetal walls. They were safe for now, but what if Erika tried to come inside. She'd never make it past Stromsky.

"Stay here." She sat Cody on a leather swivel chair, bolted to the floor. "I need to make a phone call."

Erika had to be warned. She moved over to the wall of video screens.

"Get me the first aid kit." Leon pointed to a spiral staircase on the far side of the room. "It's in the locker below."

"My friend is outside waiting for me," she said. "I have to stop her from coming in here."

"That can wait." Leon pulled a knife from his gray flack-jacket and cut Jarod's polo shirt down the front. Blood drenched his chest. The wound wasn't in his shoulder. It was over his left lung.

"I need to make this call," she said. "Now how do I work this?"

"If we don't stop the bleeding, he'll die." He pushed on the wound. "Please, I'd do it myself, but I can't take the pressure off."

"I won't leave her out there for Stromsky."

"What did you say?" He glared at her.

"I won't leave her out there." She picked up the phone and held it to her ear. No dial tone. "Where's the power?"

"Who's Stromsky?" Leon put a hand on his holstered firearm.

"What are you doing?"

"Did you hire him?"

"You think I had something to do with this?"

"Answer me," Leon shouted.

"Stop it." Cody ran over and slapped his arm. The man looked surprised. He took his hand from his gun. She raced over, picked up Cody, and put him on the leather couch in the corner.

"Don't worry," she said. "Mommy's fine."

"Did you hire him?" Leon asked.

"No," she said over her shoulder.

"How do you know his name?"

"He came to see me earlier." She turned to face him. "Now I have to warn Erika, please."

"Why is he here? Who does he work for?"

"Charlotte."

"Why does Charlotte want her son dead?"

"I don't know and I don't care what that sick family wants."

"Get this straight." He pointed at her. "I don't plan on dying down here tonight. First we're going to bandage up Mr. Carmichael, and then you're going to tell me everything."

"You get this straight." She fought back her tears. "I've spent the last year in hiding, praying that this bastard wouldn't hurt us anymore. So don't think for one second that I give a shit if he bleeds to death right here. Now are you going to help me make this call or not?"

"I'm sorry for you." Leon glanced down at Jarod. "I truly am, but he's not going to die on my watch. Just get the first aid kit. When you come back up, I'll start the system. I need to call for backup, too."

"Be ready." She raced down the spiral staircase. Over to the corrugated metal locker against the far wall. Inside, she found the first aid kit. Maybe a dozen bulletproof vests hung below. For once, she was thankful for Jarod's paranoia. She took three vests and the kit, and then raced back upstairs.

"Start it up," Vivian said as she kneeled next to Leon.

"Hold here." He moved her hands to Jarod's chest.

As Leon walked over to the console, she couldn't believe that she was helping save Jarod. Mister Vincent had told Cody that they needed him. And then that bastard had tried to kill her. It was all too confusing. For the time being, Leon had made it clear though. Jarod was to live.

Leon punched in a code. All of the security monitors maintained a black screen, except one, which showed the basement of the safe room.

"What's wrong with them?" she asked, panicked that the doors would fail as well.

"Nothing." He picked up the phone receiver. "The power's still out, so there's nothing to see outside. We have a dial tone though."

After he called the police, he traded places with her. She grabbed the phone and punched in Erika's cell. Thank God. It was ringing. Two rings.

"Answer the phone," Vivian said. Please answer. Three rings.

"Viv," Erika finally said.

"Whatever you do, do not come in here."

"I'm sorry."

"Did you hear me?" Vivian said. "Don't come in here."

"And what's wrong with my company?" a man responded. She'd recognize that British accent anywhere. Stromsky already had Erika.

"Don't hurt her."

"That will depend on you, dear. I will call you back in five minutes. See that you answer the phone."

24

Vivian hung up with her stomach twisted in knots. If Erika was out there, where was Torres? Were the police already on their way? It didn't matter. They had to rescue her. That arsenal downstairs would take care of Stromsky.

"What's going on?" Leon asked.

The security monitors sprang to life. Stromsky must've needed the time to turn the estate's power back on. None of the screens showed movement.

"He's got her," she said.

"My men are on their way." He kneeled next to Jarod. "The police, too. We just have to hold out for fifteen minutes."

"She'll be dead by then," Vivian said.

"Calm down."

She took a deep breath and nearly gagged. Drenched in blood and sweat, Jarod smelled putrid. Like raw chicken left in the trash overnight. The polished black walls of molded Titanium, whatever the hell they were, seemed to trap the air.

"What are we going to do?" she asked.

Glancing over, she saw Cody curled in a ball on the leather couch. Exhausted from the day's events, he'd somehow passed out despite all this. He hadn't sucked his thumb in over a year, but he was doing it now. Should she even let him sleep with that swollen cut on his head?

"I doubt that he has a concussion." Leon seemed to read her thoughts.

"What does Stromsky want?" She began pacing. "Why isn't he calling?"

"You need to relax."

"How can you be so cold? Erika is my friend. Maybe that doesn't mean anything to you."

"Seven of my men are dead." He tore open a gauze packet with his teeth and spit out the paper. "Clint Donovan was the best man at my wedding. Sometime later tonight, I have to go see his widow and explain why Jenny and Lisa are fatherless."

So many nights, she'd prayed that Cody would never have to endure that conversation. She felt like an ass. Leon had risked his life for her and her son.

"I'm sorry."

"I understand." He wiped sweat from his lip with the back of his hand. "I do, but panicking isn't going to change our situation."

"What am I supposed to do?" she asked.

"This Stromsky wants something, or else she'd already be dead. Now I have to stop this bleeding. In the meantime, we just have to wait for his call."

He twisted a bottle of water open, poured it over Jarod's chest, and wiped sticky blood from the wound with gauze.

The phone rang.

"Keep him talking. You need to buy time until my men arrive."

She took a deep breath. Two rings. Three. Then she picked up the phone.

"What do you want?"

"Such manners, young lady." Stromsky walked into the center monitor. She recognized the library behind him. He was right outside the safe room doors, holding a cell to one ear. With his other hand, he aimed a long barreled gun off screen.

"Don't hurt her," she said.

"You didn't uphold your end of our arrangement." Stromsky looked into the camera. Even in the gray tone screen, his eyes seemed to retain their ice blue. "I instructed you about the consequences, didn't I?"

"I did everything you asked."

"You've spoken with the police. And you warned Mr. Carmichael of my arrival."

Onscreen, he turned and pulled the cell away from his face. His voice sounded distant as he said, "Over here will be fine."

Erika walked into view carrying two chairs. Her sweater was ripped at her shoulder, her hair frizzed. She set the chairs in front of the camera.

"If you touch her—"

"That will depend on you," he said.

"Whatever business you have with Jarod, I want nothing to do with it."

"Wonderful," Stromsky said. "The last time I saw Mr. Carmichael, he didn't appear to be doing so well. Death's door, as they say. Send him out, and there will be no need for this unpleasantness to continue."

"It's not that simple."

"Yes," he said. "The security guard will need some convincing."

"What guarantees do I have that you won't try to kill us if we open the door?"

"Five minutes."

The line went dead.

In the monitor, Stromsky pulled a cord from his coat pocket and began tying Erika to the chair. There was no question in her mind. She wouldn't watch her best friend, Cody's godmother, be tortured and killed. Screw the warning. With Jarod passed out and Cody asleep, no one would be able to tell Mister Vincent what they were planning. Now all she had to do now was make Leon understand.

"I think the bullet's in his lung." He finished bandaging the wound and wiped his bloody hands on his black slacks. "There's nothing more I can do. Now what does this Stromsky want?"

"He just wants Jarod."

"My company is sending out specialists," he said. "They'll be here soon. The police, too."

"It will be too late," Vivian said. "We only have five minutes. He's right outside the door."

"What do you propose?" he asked. "Stage some half-cocked rescue attempt? For all we know, there are twenty more men waiting for us outside."

"He said if we give up Jarod," she whispered. "Then nobody else needs to die."

"Absolutely not." Leon shook his head vigorously. "I won't kill the man I'm sworn to protect."

"There's nothing you can do," she said. "Look at him. He's going to die anyway."

"That's not for me to decide."

"For once in his life," she said. "Let Jarod do something decent. Let him die for his son."

"This has nothing to do with Cody."

"The hell it doesn't. You were at the hospital that night. You saw my baby hooked up to that respirator."

"What you're talking about is murder to save our asses."

"You know what a monster Jarod is." She pointed to the wall of monitors. Center screen, Erika was bound to the chair. Dressed in all black, Stromsky sat next to her with his legs crossed. "She's studying to be a doctor. On the weekends, she helps addicts rebuild their lives."

"This man isn't some amateur," he said. "Do you think he'll just let us go?"

"He said he only wants Jarod."

"The second that we open those doors, he'll try to come in. You don't want someone like that anywhere near your son."

"We can see everything that's happening out there," she said. "If he tries anything, we shut the door."

"I can't." His voice softened, and she knew he wanted to do it. He just needed a reason.

"You should know what kind of man you're protecting." She hoped his religious rhetoric upstairs wasn't for show. "After Jarod found us last night, he murdered three teenage boys in front of Cody and me. He killed my sister Tammy, too."

"Bullshit," Leon said.

"I wouldn't lie to you about that."

"I was with him here. All day and night."

"If he was here like you say, then when did he find the time to take Cody from me?"

Leon stared down at Jarod's broken body. He walked over, sat down on the couch, and scratched his crew cut.

"He's a murderer," she said.

The phone rang. Then again.

"Please," Vivian said. "It's the right thing."

Leon stood and walked over to the console.

"If we're going to do this," he said. "I need to speak with Stromsky."

As he picked up the receiver, she prayed for a break. Just one. She glanced at Cody, who slept soundly.

Please, don't let Mister Vincent find out what we're about to do.

25

Blurred lights flickered overhead. Jarod leaned forward and rubbed a kink from his neck. Where was he? Glancing around, he found himself sitting in a row of molded plastic chairs, linked together on a steel lattice. Trapped inside the greasy light panel above, a dancing moth cast tense shadows over the Greyhound Bus Station sign.

Had he blacked out again? They were headed to the safe room with Leon. And then he woke up here.

A sparse scattering of people stood throughout the station. Though the sound of laughter and murmurs swirled around, nobody's lips moved. Was he dreaming?

In the distance, a scratchy recording of Ave Maria played. Fuck he hated that song. They only played it at funerals.

Directly across from him, a twenty-something skinhead stored an electric guitar case underneath his seat.

"Where are we?" Jarod asked. The musician's face looked as though it had been wiped with a busboy's filthy rag. Prison-ink stained the sides of his neck. "Dirt bag, I asked you a question."

Canned laughter erupted through the station. Still, nobody's lips moved. They just stared at him. Now he knew it was a dream. He must've passed out on the way to the safe room.

"Not too pleasant here." Jarod recognized Vincent's voice.

He turned to find the old man sitting a few feet away, in a chair that had been empty just a second before. His brown tweed suit hung from his frail body.

"Why have you brought me here?"

"It's got nothing to do with me." Vincent tapped his forefinger to his own temple. "This is your head."

"Then leave."

"Sorry son. This is the only place I can reach you now that your light's almost out."

"You'd better start making sense."

"Didn't I warn you about messing with that woman?" Vincent's nostrils flared. "Aren't too many folks stupid enough to attack a lioness. Especially one protecting her cub."

"And I told you that there was no way that bitch was going to take my son."

"That's right." Vincent nodded. "There's no way. Not one. Except right now, you're stuck here with me, and she's fixing to put you down like some mongrel dog."

"Let her try," he said. "She doesn't stand a chance."

"Now that's where you're wrong." A smug look crossed Vincent's face. "She's cutting a deal to trade you over to Mr. Kevin Stromsky as we speak."

"Impossible," Jarod said, but he wasn't so sure. No. This was another one of Vincent's power games. "Leon wouldn't let her."

"That man turned on you the second you passed out."

Could that be true? Something in Vincent's eyes told him that it was.

"I'll kill them both," Jarod said.

"Mighty tall words from a man who's lying in a puddle of his own blood."

Vincent's deliberate laugh made him furious.

"If you're here," Jarod said. "You must think you can help."

"I might be able to give you a boost," Vincent said. "Keep you awake for a second or two to stop the trade, but that bullet's in your lung. Unless your boy opens the gate for me, you're dead anyway."

"You mean like last night?" Jarod remembered the visions that Vincent had shown him in the bathroom. How he'd supposedly torn that kid's head off. Earlier, the carnage had made him sick to his stomach. Now, he only wanted one more opportunity to do the same to Vivian. "Wake me up, and I'll handle her."

"No." A stern look crossed Vincent's face. "You won't touch her."

"She shot me. I won't let her live."

"You're going to be a happy family if it kills me. You're going to make Cody feel just fine until the portal is opened. You hear me?"

"Don't speak to me like that."

"I asked you a question," Vincent said. "Do you understand?"

Jarod couldn't believe the nerve. Treating him like some grade school kid.

"I've been jumping through your hoops all day," he said. "I'm through dancing unless you tell me what you're really after."

Applause echoed through the bus station. He looked around. As he suspected, none of the people moved. They just stared at him.

"You've screwed off everything that I've done for you." Vincent bared his teeth. His gums looked diseased. "The power. The money. Everything. And now you think you can give me orders?"

"Done for me?"

"You're gonna fix this," Vincent said. "Then you will leave that woman alone."

"Without me, you wouldn't even exist," Jarod said, and Vincent's eyes widened. "What, you think I couldn't figure why you need me alive?"

"Choose your next words carefully."

"The way I see it, you'd better start treating me with some fucking respect," Jarod said. "I answer to no one."

"Oh, you will." The lights flickered to darkness. "Or you'll rot here with your mistakes."

The power returned. A slick tongue of blood led down the dirty isle to three corpses. They stared with eyes of pure black. Their lips moved, but no sound came.

Two of the boys bled from their necks. The woman's body had been torn so viciously that it seemed on the verge of collapse. The musician across the aisle held his own head in his lap.

"Christ." Jarod stood and backed away.

"What's the matter?" Vincent's guttural laugh seemed to shake the walls. "Scared of what you've done?"

"Get rid of them," he shouted.

"You still haven't learned who's giving the orders." Vincent stood.

Suddenly, the air burned oven hot. Jarod stepped back, but his shoes melted to the floor. He tripped and dropped to his hands, which blistered.

"Stop now," Jarod shouted. "Or I'll never help you."

As the old man walked, chairs rattled. Dust sprinkled from the ceiling panels.

"You were my brightest creation." Vincent touched his face with icy fingers that stabbed into Jarod's cheek like needles. "And now the great Jarod Carmichael dies on his knees."

"Wait." He clutched the old man's pant leg to avoid the floor, which began to glow red. "Don't leave me."

"Why would I waste my time on you? Somebody who is broken beyond repair. Somebody who answers to no one." He mocked Jarod's voice.

"I'll do what you want. Don't let me die."

"Before you ever open your mouth to me again." Vincent leaned down just inches from his face. "Choose your words."

"I will." He was disgusted with his own weakness, but he couldn't stop begging. "I'll do what you want. Anything. Don't leave me here."

"You have one last chance. That's your son. Either he opens the doorway for me, or you die. It's that simple."

A sharp pain exploded in Jarod's ribcage. Suddenly, he wasn't in the bus depot anymore. With blurred vision, he looked up to see a woman's face. Lines morphed and folded together, and he could barely make out Vivian, struggling to carry him by his arms. Leon lifted his legs.

"Let go of me." His dried tongue stuck to the roof of his mouth.

"He's conscious," Leon said.

"It doesn't matter," the bitch said. "I'm not leaving Erika out there."

Jarod could barely see Vincent standing beside the console.

"Take the gun from her waist band," he said. "Shoot the guard." The sound of pistons releasing. Was that the door to the safe room?

"You'd better hurry," Vincent said. "Not much time left."

Jarod reached for the gun, grabbed it, and aimed wildly in Leon's direction. He pulled the trigger. Immediately, his legs dropped. He pulled away from Vivian.

From nowhere, he found the energy to stand. She raced over to him and shoved her finger into his bullet wound, but he felt no pain. He slammed the butt of the pistol across her head and kicked her through the doors of the safe room. Quickly, he locked himself back inside. On the floor next to him, he saw the bullet had hit Leon in the face. It served him right. The fucking traitor

Cody was crying on the far side of the room.

"Open it." Jarod staggered to him. "Open the doorway for Mister Vincent."

Cody shook his head, so Jarod pointed to the monitors over the center console.

"If you want to save your mother." He coughed thick blood into his hands. "If you want to save—" He paused. "Your mother, you have to let Vincent." More breaths. "Let him in."

Jarod fell. He felt strangely disconnected from his body.

"Bad Daddy." Cody's voice echoed through the static. "You're bad."

26

Jarod's punch felt like an aluminum bat to Vivian's skull. Her ears rang. As she staggered back to the vault, the doors wheezed shut. Cody was trapped inside. Was Leon alive? Most of the bullets had hit his vest, but at least one had hit his face. She had to get back inside.

A cold barrel pressed to the base of her skull.

"It seems that you've failed to live up to the terms of our agreement yet again." Stromsky's voice felt like a wire around her neck.

Slowly, she turned. He wore a black suit and leather gloves. His eyes bore down on her with such anger, that she was forced to look away.

"I tried to give him to you." She could barely open her mouth to speak. Her jaw throbbed from the punch.

"Move over there," he said.

He nudged her and she walked. The back half of the library came into view. Turned on its side, Jarod's desk was riddled with bullet holes. Beyond that, two wrought iron chairs were arranged in the center of the room. Erika sat in the farthest one with her hands tied behind her back. Her right eye was swollen shut. Blood trickled from the corner of her lip.

"I warned you of the consequences for speaking to the authorities," Stromsky said. "Now sit."

"I didn't say anything to them."

Pain exploded over her left ear. She fell into a potted palm tree. Spiny fronds dug into her hands.

"I shouldn't have to repeat myself," he said.

Why didn't he just kill them? Jarod wasn't going to open the doors. She sat down, and he pulled several plastic ties from his pocket.

"I'll make this simple for you." Stromsky walked around her. Somehow, he managed to restrain her hands behind the chair without taking the barrel of the gun from her head. "When matters become complicated, my employers begin to question my qualifications to complete the job."

"I just want my son."

"Because of your actions, Mrs. Carmichael has commissioned a second team." Stromsky grabbed a handful of Erika's curls and yanked her head back.

"Leave her alone," Vivian shouted.

"I will not have my reputation tarnished." He holstered his gun underneath his black jacket and checked his watch. "You have just under five minutes until they arrive." He motioned to the vault doors. "Either give me access to Mr. Carmichael so I can clean up this debacle, or matters will become unpleasant for you both."

Leon had gained them access to the room. If Stromsky knew that she didn't have the code, would he shoot them right there? Yes. She needed to buy time for the police to arrive.

"What guarantees do I have that you'll set us free?" Vivian asked.

"Don't," Erika said quietly. "He's going to frame you for Jarod's murder."

"I assure you that I'm only after Mr. Carmichael," Stromsky said. "Four and a half minutes."

"I overheard him on the phone," Erika slurred. "They want to take Cody from you."

"I can see that we're not communicating," Stromsky said. He'd used those exact words when he'd nearly broken her wrist in the hospital. "Did you know that the human thumb accounts for forty percent of all hand function?" He reached into his pocket and pulled out something. God, no. Wire cutters.

"Don't do this," Vivian said.

As he kneeled behind Erika's chair, she just stared forward with half-closed eyes.

"In fact," Stromsky said. "Its importance is such, that I've read in the World Journal of Surgery that surgeons have reattached the big toe to the hand when the thumb has been severed." He pulled open the clamps. Erika's breath became quick and shallow. "A filthy practice to say the least, but it demonstrates just how important this particular digit is."

"I'll help you get Jarod," Vivian said. "Whatever you want. I already shot him once myself. He's almost dead."

Stromsky stopped and looked at her. "The code."

"I can't give you Cody—"

The sound of splitting bone filled her ears. Erika wretched forward. Her scream raked down Vivian's spine. Her thumb dropped onto the wood floors.

"You motherfucker," Vivian shouted and struggled with her bonds.

"Don't worry." Stromsky looked at his watch. "Four minutes is plenty of time for you as well."

Where were the police? They should have been here by now. Rivers of tears streaked Erika's cheeks, bordered by banks of black mascara. She whimpered, her chin hanging down.

"The middle finger is not quite as useful," Stromsky said. "But I assure you, combined with the loss of the thumb, the hand can appear quite hideous."

Now, Vivian knew. They were going to die unless she did something.

"Promise me that you won't hurt Cody," she said.

"Don't," Erika said.

"Young lady, I hardly think you're in any position to give orders."

"Promise me," Vivian said, desperate for any time. "Or I'll never tell you—"

The crunch of a second finger. Vivian screamed at him. She pulled at her restraints. Her chair screeched across the hardwood floor, but her arms wouldn't budge. Looking over, she saw Erika's head slumped forward. On the floor behind her chair, two of her fingers sat in a growing puddle of blood.

"I swear to God I'm going to kill you," Vivian said.

"No, no, no." Stromsky clicked his tongue. "This won't do."

"You'll have to kill me because I'll never give you my son. Do you hear me you fuck?"

Stromsky pulled out his gun. "Are you certain?"

"Never," she screamed so loud, her voice cut out.

"So reckless with a friend's life." He held the gun to Erika's temple. She looked over and mouthed the words *I love you.*

Vivian's eyes welled up.

"How touching," Stromsky said.

If they were going to die tonight, she'd give the prick something to remember her by. Vivian spit in his face.

Frantically, he wiped his eyes with his sleeve.

Vivian grasped the spokes of the chair, stood, and spun around. In her mind, she'd hoped to knock Stromsky down, but the chair barely struck him. From behind, somebody tackled her. She crashed to the floor. Pain shot through her shoulder.

"Don't move," a man shouted and pushed down on her head.

Trapped on her side, three more sets of black boots danced sideways around her face. Were they the police? Or the second team that Stromsky had been talking about?

"Where is he?" the same voice shouted. "Where's Jarod?"

"The little weasel has locked himself in the safe room," Stromsky said.

"Secure." Another man aimed a machine gun at Erika.

"We have this covered." A soldier with slits for eyes handed Stromsky back his gun. "Mrs. Carmichael is waiting for your call."

For a moment, she had hoped for some way through this mess. These men weren't going to help her. They worked for the same people who'd hired that psychopath to kidnap her baby. At least Cody was safe inside the panic room. Stromsky looked furious.

"You have two choices," the voice above her said. "Give us the code now, or we shoot you and blow open the doors." He cocked a gun and pressed the barrel to her cheek. "You have five seconds to decide."

❦❦❦

Leon clawed himself along the rubber mats. His ribs were broken, his face on fire from the gunshot. As he breathed, blood and drool leaked down his chin. Somewhere, a child cried. It had to be Cody, but he couldn't worry about him now.

He latched onto the center console. It took all of his strength just to pull himself up. In the shattered monitor, four men secured the library outside. Christ, thank you Lord. The police had arrived.

The five feet to the door release might as well have been a thousand, but he would reach it. Never before had he wanted to see Nina so badly. He began inching along. He would give her that ring. Take her to Vegas in the morning if he had to. Tonight, he was going to live.

24

D o you understand what I'm saying?" The soldier grabbed Vivian's neck with a rough hand. He pressed her head to the floor and leaned close to her ear. "You will die unless you give me the code."

"You won't murder my son." She struggled to get free, but her hands were still tied to the chair behind her back.

"Mr. Boothe," Stromsky said. "I assure you that this won't do. Now kindly step aside and let me finish my work."

"There isn't time," Boothe said. "The police will be here soon."

"We're all over the scanner." Another soldier moved close. With her cheekbone crushed against the hardwood floor, she could only see his scuffed boots, caked in mud. "The locals are on their way."

"You've really screwed this one to hell, old man," Boothe said. "Blow the door."

Were they going to use explosives? Leon had said that the room was just a deterrent. Visions of Cody wandering through the smoke, deafened from the blast filled her mind.

"Wait," she said, desperate for any extra time. "I'll open it."

"The code," Boothe said. "Now."

"Four…seventeen…nineteen—"

"The panel is alpha numeric." Someone cut her off. "She's lying."

"No, wait." She'd hoped to buy at least a minute. "Please. I just have to *see* the keypad."

"Freeze," another deep voice called out. "Don't fucking move."

For an eternity, voices shouted in every direction. With the floorboard vibrating against her ear, it sounded like an army was marching.

In her peripheral view, she saw movement. She never thought she'd be so happy to see Detective Torres. He took cover behind a grandfather clock.

Boothe cut her hands free. As he yanked her between himself and the police, a pock-faced soldier grabbed Erika. Dozens of police officers in riot gear stormed the room. All seemed to be aiming at Vivian's head. She looked around. Stromsky was nowhere to be seen. In the confusion, the bastard had managed to slip away.

"Stay back," Boothe shouted at the cops. He signaled with his hand. The other soldiers moved into formation. Two held Erika and Vivian forward as shields, while the remaining two ducked low behind. All of them aimed their laser-scoped rifles at the cops. "Get back now. Or these two die."

"It doesn't have to go down like this," Torres said.

As the police closed in, Erika made eye contact. Afraid to touch her hand, Vivian reached out and held her wrist.

"Clear a path." Boothe shoved Vivian forward. He held the barrel to her temple. "You have five seconds."

The power shut off again. Somehow, Stromsky must've made it down to the cellar. Was he trying to escape? Or was he trying to even his odds of killing everyone. Flashlights pierced the darkness, blinding her.

A muffled rhythm grew louder. She looked up just as a spotlight beamed down through the glass ceiling. A helicopter swung close.

"Four," Boothe shouted. "Three."

"Nobody has to get hurt today," Torres shouted. "Please."

"Two."

To her right, a piston wheezed. Somebody was opening the panic room doors. Cody would be exposed.

For a moment, everyone seemed to forget that their weapons were pointed at each other. They stared as Leon crawled into the spotlight on his elbows. His face was mangled. Where was Jarod? Had he died? And what about Cody? She tried to pull away to find him. Boothe yanked on her hair and snapped her head back.

"Close the doors," Vivian shouted at Leon. "It's not safe."

He stopped just as Jarod staggered from the darkness. All flashlights moved to him as he fell against the doorjamb. His back spasmed, shoving his chest forward. All of his muscles twitched violently. Two curved bone spikes, six inches long, sprouted from the backs of his elbows. It was too late. He was changing.

"Stop him," Vivian shouted at the police.

Jarod's jaw unhinged, ripping his cheeks to his ears. Jagged bone shards punched through his gums and shoved his bloodied teeth onto the floor in front of him. Immediately, he began clinking his new incisors together.

"Jesus fucking Christ," someone behind her said.

"You're here to kill him," Vivian yelled at Boothe. "Do it."

"If we open fire," he said. "They will, too."

"Making deals with my life." Jarod looked down at Leon. Vivian stared in horror as he stepped on Leon's back, latched finger hooks around his neck, and tore his head free. A segment of spine and muscle tissue, still connected to the head, glistened in the flashlight beams. Oh God. Leon's lips still moved.

"Dammit," Vivian shouted. "He's going to kill us."

"Yes." Jarod's head snapped to the side. He stared directly at her with reflective eyes of mercury. "But don't worry, butterfly. I've got something special planned for you."

Gunfire erupted. He turned to climb the bookcase. The police and the mercenaries seemed forget about the standoff. They all began shooting at the monster.

As Jarod scaled the walls, his body writhed side-to-side. Bullets tore chunks from his flesh, but he kept climbing, until he disappeared into pitchy darkness.

Then came the screams.

28

Vivian ducked the flashlight beams that swept every direction. She pulled Erika behind an overturned table. The wrought iron barely provided any cover from the storm of machine gun fire all around.

"I have to get Cody," she said

"I'm fine." Erika scooted back on the floor and leaned against the overturned desk.

Vivian darted for the doors. Boothe stepped back into her path, firing at the ceiling. She bounced off his body and slammed to the floor.

He swung his weapon around and aimed at her head. For a second, he seemed to consider what to do.

Above, the police helicopter veered back over the glass ceiling. He covered his eyes from the spotlight. Seizing the moment, she stood and raced around him through the vault doors. More gunfire behind. Was he shooting at her?

Glancing back, she found that he'd turned his attention back to Jarod.

Inside, Cody slept on the couch where she'd left him. His shallow breaths sounded like gasps for air. She ran to his side, knelt, and kissed his sweaty forehead. He was burning up in the reddish glow of the room's running lights.

"Baby." She shook him gently to make sure he wasn't hurt. "I'm here."

"Mary, Mary, quite contrary." His eyes shot open, exposing only the white. "How does your garden grow?"

She felt sick. Though he couldn't pronounce most of the words, she knew the nursery rhyme about Mary Tudor. Bloody Mary.

"It's okay, sweetie." She picked up his limp body. "Mommy will fix it."

Now, she knew more than ever—whatever had transformed Jarod was changing Cody, too. But into what? Was it genetic? It didn't matter. No doctor or scientist could fix the spikes growing from Jarod's body. Nor could they explain Mister Vincent. Cody needed a priest. An exorcism. Something.

She carried him to the door.

"Stay back," a man cried out. Maybe thirty feet away, his scream ended in a choking sound. Less than five minutes had passed, but the gunfire had grown sparse. Despite their armor, weapons, and numbers, the LAPD were losing to Jarod. If she didn't leave now, they wouldn't be able to.

She clutched Cody and ran, taking the long way down a bookshelf aisle to avoid gunfire. Around the corner, she found Erika still leaned against the desk.

"Is he hurt?" she asked.

"He's sleeping." Vivian prayed she wouldn't hear his whispered chants. At least his eyes were closed now. "The keys to Jarod's garage are in the kitchen. Can you make it?"

"I'm ready." Erika's knees wobbled as she stood.

Keeping along the outside walls of the library, they began moving to the exit. Then Vivian noticed the quiet. No one was shooting anymore. Or screaming.

They exited the library into the estate's main corridor. She looked down and gagged. Several discarded flashlights shined skewed beams of light across the blood-drenched stone tile. Torn limbs and discarded weapons littered the room, but the police officer's bodies were nowhere to be seen.

"We're not going to make it out of here," Erika said.

"Don't say that." Vivian steadied her footing on the slippery floor. "Are you able to carry Cody?"

Using her good arm, Erika took him from her. Vivian tried not to look at the gristled elbow socket as she stepped on a forearm and pried a machine gun from its grip. She hung the strap over her neck. The attached flashlight aimed where the gun did. Down the hallway, police lights flashed through the row of arched stone windows. No sirens.

"Silver bells and cockleshells," Cody said.

"You're so brave," Erika said quietly. "My tough little man."

"When we get to the front door," Vivian whispered. "I need you to get Cody to safety."

"Jarod just killed all of those men. What do you think you're gonna do?"

"I'm not trying to stop him, but I can't go to the police yet." They didn't have time to argue. If the cops decided to lock her up, it might be too late to save Cody from whatever was inside of him. "Get him outside the estate. I'll find you later tonight."

"I won't leave you." Erika shook her head.

"And I won't let you leave," Jarod said from above.

"Go," Vivian shouted. "Don't let him get Cody."

Something splashed the flashlight lens. Aiming the gun up, she gasped. Ten feet above her head, an officer's corpse dangled by his feet from the chandelier. Blood dripped down his outstretched arms. As he swayed, shadows moved behind him. At least two other dead bodies had also been fastened in a row.

To her left, she heard something. Jarod's body contorted in jerky movements as he crawled across the wall. She fired. The weapon's recoil kicked a trail of bullets across his body, and up an oil painting. Looking back, she saw Erika run out the front door.

"It looks like we're finally alone." He climbed down to the ground and stood. Police lights pulsed over his body as he passed in front of a window. He looked outside. "They won't make it far."

"I won't let you take my son." She tried to take his attention from Cody. "Do you hear me, limp dick?"

"He's not for me." Jarod's disfigured jaw formed a permanent grin. "I can't wait to see the look on your face when it happens to him."

"He's not like you. He'll never be like you."

"No." His shout vibrated her chest. "He'll never be me."

He leapt forward, and she fired. The bullet tore away a chunk of his skull. And then he was on her. She struggled to fight him, but he sank his claws into her shoulder. Her arm felt like it was being torn off.

"You thought you were so fucking smart hiding from me." His breath made her gag. "Didn't you?"

"Get off—" She could barely talk. "Me."

"Didn't you?" He pulled her head to the side and hissed. "He's coming soon. It's going to burn. They're all going to scream."

He twisted his claws in her shoulder and bit down on her neck. Searing pain branched through her body. Please God, just let Erika get away.

Then he pulled off her and howled in apparent pain. She could barely turn her head.

"She's mine," Jarod shouted at no one.

Mister Vincent was here. She knew it. And from the conversation, it sounded like he still wanted her alive. But why? For Cody's sake? It had to be.

"I'll do anything." She choked out the words. "Just don't let him hurt my son."

More gunfire erupted, punching Jarod's body. A blur of legs ran past her. Someone helped her to her feet.

Immediately, she tried to run after Cody and Erika, but she stumbled.

"Vivian," a voice said. She looked up to find Detective Torres. Somehow, he'd survived. "It's okay."

"Stop him," she told him. "He's going after Cody."

"Our backup just arrived," Torres said. "He's a dead man."

"You don't understand," she said. Glass shattered down the hallway. She pulled away from Torres and stumbled to the front door. "You're too late. He can't be killed now."

29

Vivian raced onto the front balcony. A large beam of light stopped her cold. On the lawn, dozens of officers took cover behind their open car doors with their weapons aimed at her. Behind a row of sculpted bushes, more gunfire rattled.

Finally. The police were chasing Jarod. Could she trust them? Not yet. There was still too much confusion. Besides, an army couldn't protect her from that monster. She needed to find Erika and disappear before Jarod had a chance to regroup.

"Drop your weapon," someone said over a PA system.

"Hold your fire." Detective Torres pulled her back. "She's one of the hostages."

"Get your hands off me," she said.

"You're going to get yourself killed." He unstrapped the gun from her neck.

"Where's my son?" She moved into a torrential downpour that drenched her with freezing rain.

Torres followed behind. "Slow down."

"I warned you what was going to happen."

"You need medical attention."

Although her shoulder and neck ached from Jarod's bite, her strength was returning. Two officers raced forward. They smothered her with a blanket and pulled her across the waterlogged grass, behind the line of police cars.

"Get a medic over here," Torres said to them.

"I'm fine," she said. "Just find Jarod."

"SWAT is on it. That cop killer won't make it through the night."

"You're wrong," she told him. "You need to warn your men that Jarod can't be killed now."

"What are you talking about?"

"I just shot him in the head, and that didn't stop him."

A strange look crossed his face. Screw him if he thought she was crazy. He must've seen Jarod's transformation. Only an idiot wouldn't listen now.

All around, haphazard cars parked with their siren lights flashing. Officers ran every direction.

"Where is my son?" she demanded.

"Being evacuated." He pointed to a helicopter that had landed on the grass in the middle of the circular driveway. "I don't want you to panic, but we're flying him to Trinity Medical."

"What?" she asked. "What happened?"

Rain poured over his face. He looked as though he didn't know what to say, but she already knew the answer.

He's coming soon.

She turned and splashed across the lawn. Mister Vincent was coming. There was no doubt that's what Jarod had meant.

She raced under the wind of the helicopter's whipping blades. Torres opened the rear door. Inside the fuselage, Erika held Cody in the far window seat with her right hand raised. It was wrapped in gauze. Another officer, who barely looked old enough to drink, sat behind her. In the cockpit, the pilot flipped some switches and muttered into his headset.

"Thank God," Erika said.

"What's going on?" Vivian stepped into the cargo hold. "Is he hurt?"

"Little man," Erika said over the high-pitched whine of the engines. "Mommy's here."

Vivian took him from her. His eyes were still closed, but he was hyperventilating.

"It's okay, sweetie." She dried his hair with the police blanket wrapped around his body.

"They tried to take him from me." Erika flashed the cop in the backseat a dirty look.

"You three will be safe now," Torres said.

"Jarod," Vivian told him. "Warn your men."

"We're on it," he said, but she could tell he wasn't really listening. He turned to the officer behind her. "Their lives are in your hands, Franklin."

He slid the rear door shut and slapped the chassis.

As the helicopter lifted off, she kissed Cody's forehead. They knew about Jarod now. The police knew, but what could she do about Mister Vincent?

"Cody's strong." Erika had always been able to read her mind.

"I know, it's just—" She blinked back her tears. "I don't even know what we're dealing with. And now that Jarod's changed, I don't think he can be killed."

"Back inside, you told that white-haired prick that you'd shot Jarod. That he was almost dead, right?"

"I put a bullet in his lung. I thought for sure he was gone."

"That doesn't sound too invincible to me."

"My God," Vivian said. So much had happened, she hadn't had time to put it together. The only reason she didn't kill Jarod earlier tonight was because of Cody.

"He'll change back soon enough," Erika said. "Just like before."

"Next time," Vivian said. "I'll put one between his eyes."

The helicopter dipped, leveled off, and vibrated. She looked out the windshield. Ahead, dark storm clouds formed a massive funnel. Lightning branched at its epicenter. Miles below, several freeways formed thin veins of light that crisscrossed the terrain.

"Nothing to worry about," Officer Franklin said behind her. "Just a little turbulence."

"How close are we to the hospital?" she asked the pilot, but he didn't respond. "Excuse me." She leaned forward and tapped his shoulder.

"Soon." He barely turned his head. Something felt wrong. Then she noticed his hair creeping from underneath his helmet. It was white. Immediately, she turned to Franklin.

"I have to see his face," she said.

"What's going on?" Erika asked.

"The pilot," Vivian said. "He tried to kill us tonight."

"Ted Riley has been with the department since I was a kid," Franklin said.

"It's not Ted Riley," Vivian told him.

"You need to calm down," he said.

"Don't tell us to calm down." Erika turned around. "Do your damn job."

"Fine." Officer Franklin crouched and moved to the front of the cab. He spoke to the pilot, who unstrapped his helmet and pulled it off. The middle-aged man looked back with a round face and moist eyes. His hair hadn't even grayed. It was blond.

"I'm sorry," she said.

"It's been a long night." Officer Franklin waved it away and retook his seat. "Better to be safe."

Something popped behind her. Wind began whipping her hair. The engines roared. She spun around and saw the back window was missing.

A blur skittered past the window. She pulled Erika toward the center of the cab.

"What is it?" Erika asked.

"Something's outside." Vivian set Cody on the floor and covered him with her body.

"Both of you stay down." Franklin pulled his gun and spun around, aiming at every window.

"What's going on?" the pilot yelled back. "What happened?"

"Find a place to set down." Franklin held onto straps that were connected to the roof for balance.

Vivian strained to see any movement. Every few seconds, lightning branched around them, and she realized that they were approaching the storm's epicenter. Suddenly, Jarod's face filled the window. He somehow clung to the outside of the fuselage.

"Behind you," Erika shouted.

Jarod punched out the glass, dug his claw underneath Franklin's chin, and yanked him. Vivian grabbed his feet, but they slipped from her grasp. He disappeared out the window. Jarod, too, was nowhere to be seen.

Underneath the cab, muffled sounds of shearing metal. Was Jarod tearing the helicopter apart? That didn't make sense. If they crashed, everyone could die. Mister Vincent wanted Cody alive. Didn't he?

"How far until the hospital?" Vivian shouted over the whine of wind and engine.

"Ten minutes," Riley said.

"Can we call for backup?" She picked up Franklin's gun from the floor.

"The radio's down," Riley said. "I can't make contact."

The lights of civilization converged along the dark coastline ahead of them. Was that Santa Barbara? Ventura? It didn't matter. Their lives depended on reaching that city.

"Shit," Riley said. "The oil pressure is dropping. I have to make an emergency landing."

"You can't put this down." She realized Jarod's plan. Crashing the helicopter wasn't the goal. If so, why not just kill the pilot? He was forcing them to land. "We have to get to civilization or he'll kill us all."

"This isn't a plane," Riley shouted. "We'll drop like stone when the engines fail. That's if the weather doesn't take us out first."

"Then fly close to the beach. We can set down there if we have to."

"Fuck me!" He jerked back in his chair.

Through the windshield, she saw Jarod's talon latch onto the hood from underneath the nose section. He gripped the helicopter's metal skin, shredding it like clay.

Almost every second now, lightning strobed his body. His shoeless feet, with those same fishhook claws, left a trail of puncture marks torn through the metal in his wake as he climbed up the nose section.

"Stay low in case we crash," Vivian shouted. She raised her gun but didn't dare take the shot. The turbulence was too severe. What if the bullet struck the rotor blades?

Jarod clutched the hood with two feet and an arm. He reared back and punched the Plexiglas windscreen back against Riley, who banked hard right. The chopper tilted sideways.

Erika held Cody in her arms as she slid. Lodged between the seats, Vivian held them both against the floor. A first aid kit fell through the missing side window, just inches from Erika's feet. The helicopter righted.

"He's still on board," Riley shouted.

Looking up, she saw four gashes had shredded the hood. Jarod's hand seemed to barely hang from the side.

"How far to the hospital?" She looked ahead. Her eyes watered in the wind. They were actually flying over buildings now.

"Maybe a minute," he said.

"Can we make it?"

Jarod punched through the door and swiped at Riley.

Vivian held the barrel of her gun against his wrist and fired. He withdrew. The helicopter began to shudder. Ahead, the hospital's landing pad was deserted.

"Get ready," Riley said.

Jittering back and forth in the downpour, they began to descend over the helipad. Thirty feet.

"We're going to make a break." Vivian moved back into the cargo hold next to Erica and said, "Jump out first. Then I'll hand Cody to you."

"What about you?"

"I'll be behind you." She motioned to the gun. "I need my hands free."

Erika slid open the door. Vivian peeked outside but couldn't see Jarod anywhere.

Ten feet above the helipad, they hovered. Erika leapt down. Vivian picked up Cody and prepared to hand him over.

Jarod crawled up from the belly of the helicopter. She tried to aim at him, but he pierced her forearm with his hooks. Pain coursed through her wrist. He snatched Cody from her and shoved her through the door.

A blur of lights. She slammed down onto the rooftop, the wind knocked from her lungs. Rain splattered her face as she stared up. The helicopter began to ascend again. Jarod still hung from outside the helicopter, clutching Cody by his collar, dangling him outside the fuselage like a rag doll.

Above, the storm funnel had swallowed the sky. It began spiraling faster.

The helicopter veered right, then left. They were two stories up now. She stood and staggered toward them. The chopper dipped again. Her stomach leapt into her throat.

"Mommy," Cody cried out.

God, at some point, he'd woken from that trance.

"Baby." She choked out the word.

His collar ripped and he fell. She sprinted forward and caught him. His momentum shoved them both to the floor. Luckily, she managed to shield his fall with her body.

"Cody." She hugged him, and then checked his body for cuts or breaks. "Baby, can you hear me. Are you hurt?"

"Mommy," he shouted. His eyes snapped open. Though she was directly in front of him, he didn't seem to see her.

"Cody." She shook him hard. "Baby. God, anyone. I don't know what to do."

He grabbed her cheeks. Pain needles stabbed her head. Every hair, her ears and eyes felt as though they were ripped from her skull. Her arms went numb, then her spine and legs.

The world began to disintegrate.

30

Vivian's head felt as though it was squeezed through a garden hose. The hospital rooftop, the helicopter, Cody and the hurricane all blinked away into blurred colors, which slowly focused. She found herself alone on a street, maybe fifty-feet wide, formed from diamond-shaped cobblestones in varying shades of blue. The orange sky burned too brightly as well, swirled in fluorescent pink.

On either side of the road, a forest of dead trees locked branches in a tangle of bramble and mud that seemed impassable. Giant mantises and other hook-armed insects flitted and scurried about. None crossed the invisible street barrier though. She turned. Behind her, the cobblestones stopped, leaving only a muddy, rutted road that choked off into the charred forest.

Was she dead? Passed out on the roof? No. Somehow, Cody had brought her here when he touched her face, but where was this? Some kind of dream maybe. Was this where he went when his eyes were rolled back white? If that was the case, where was he? She had to hurry and find him. Jarod was back on the roof, trying to kill them right now.

"Cody," Vivian yelled and turned back around.

Dead center in the street, a wooden rocking horse as large as a Clydesdale appeared. Its wide eyes and painted smile sent chills through her as it wobbled back and forth.

"Cody," she yelled again.

"Are you lost?" said a voice in a Cockney accent. A brunette girl with a single braid over her shoulder stood beside the wooden horse. Her yellow dress seemed to match the smell of lemon squares and chocolate, Cody's two favorite treats.

"My son." Vivian walked over to her. "Where's Cody?"

The girl shrugged.

"Don't lie to me. I know he's here."

"You're not supposed to be here, you know." The girl reached up and began combing the horse's red yarn mane. A black golf ball-sized welt with freckles had sprouted on the side of her neck. "You should go home. Cody lives with us now."

"Cody," Vivian shouted. "Where are you, baby."

"Shhh." The girl tried to grab her hand, and she flinched. "He'll come back."

"Who will come back? Mister Vincent?"

The girl shook her head violently and stared behind her. Vivian turned. The horse no longer rocked. Its painted nostrils seemed more flared than before, its smile gone.

"Don't say his name," the girl said.

"Mommy," Cody yelled from far off.

"Stay away from them, baby." Vivian charged down the street toward him. "Don't touch them."

Within seconds, she came upon a massive circular clearing made of that same cobblestone. At the center, a house had been built from blue Legos, the roof in red. Around the perimeter of the clearing, dozens more life-sized toys seemed to stand guard. Elmo and plastic Pikachu. Optimus Prime's forearm was missing. In fact, most of the toys had one limb or another severed, and yet they all smiled.

Just feet away, guarding the house's front picket fence, Cody's stuffed bear stood taller than she did, wearing a British Royal Guard hat. It held a musket, with one claw wrapped around the barrel. Patches of its fur had been rubbed off, exposing raw skin, mottled with blood. That hanging eye dangled as turned its head, following her.

Inside the perimeter of toys, a group of children formed a rotating circle with their hands locked. The' girls' frilled dresses whipped as they danced. The' boys' cowboy boots clicked on the granite tiles. Open sores. Scabs. Scar tissue. All of them diseased in different ways.

"Ring a ring of roses," they chanted.

Vivian ran up. They stopped and stared at her.

"Mommy." Cody's voice sounded like it came from the Lego house.

"Move out of my way," Vivian told the kids.

"Mommy," the children said, but their mouths didn't move. "Go away. You can't be here."

"I'm never leaving," Vivian shouted at Mister Vincent. "Do you hear me? You'll have to kill me."

An earthquake shook the street. The tiles crumbled and ruptured a two-inch gap that led to her feet. She jumped to one side. The kids scattered and hid behind the toys.

"It's not smart to mess with things once they're in motion." The raspy voice sounded much too friendly.

An elderly black man emerged from the trees. Mister Vincent. He had to be. His moth-eaten suit hung from his frail body. No doubt his jaundiced eyes and wrinkled skin were a mask. But a mask for what? What could possibly turn Jarod into that creature?

"I want my son," she told him.

"You're only making this worse for him."

"Give him back. Now."

"Watch how you speak." His voice grew quiet. "We don't have to do this the easy way."

All around, the toys began twitching and moaning. She didn't dare find out what would happen if she pushed too hard. First, she had to get Cody. Then they could worry about escaping.

"I'm sorry," she said. "Please, I have to talk to my son."

"Just you being here has already gotten him worked up." He motioned behind her at Cody's bear, which pulled fur from its own shoulder with sharpened teeth.

"That's disgusting," Vivian said. "You let my son see this?"

"Just where do you think you are?" he asked.

"I don't care about whatever twisted jollies you get in here, but—"

"I couldn't do this if I wanted to. Here in Cody Town, he makes the rules. It would be wise if you helped me calm him. Otherwise, things could get real messy for everyone."

"You're lying," she told him, but deep down she wasn't sure. She recognized everything here from Cody's toy box.

"This oasis, these soldiers are the only things holding back the nasty thoughts." He motioned to a two-foot millipede just beyond the walkway. A crow perched on its back, pecking out bits of its intestine.

"I know you're lying now. My baby is not creating that."

"With the way you and Jarod have been carrying on, are you really that surprised that the boy's got some issues to work through?"

"You turned Jarod into that thing. Do you have any idea of what he's doing out there right now?"

"You'll have to forgive me, but I've been a bit busy here. Lots of preparations and all."

"He's trying to kill me."

"Yes, well." Mister Vincent gave a knowing nod and scratched a patch of his scraggly beard. "Probably you shouldn't have shot him in the chest earlier tonight."

"He tried to murder Cody, too."

"I'm sure that's not true."

"Really," she said. "He just dropped him from a helicopter."

His jaw clenched and he looked down. Could it be? Last night, Mister Vincent had told Cody Jay-Jay's name, so she'd assumed that he was all knowing. A ghost or a demon or something.

This news had clearly caught him by surprise though. What did that mean? That he had to be present in order to know the things he knew? The hairs on her neck rose. She'd only been fourteen when she babysat Jay-Jay. Years before she'd even met Jarod. How long had Mister Vincent been watching her?

"What do you want from us?"

"I already told you," he said. "Calm your son. Make him happy. Then I'll help send you home safe and sound."

"And I just told you that Jarod is out there right now trying to kill us. We're running out of time."

"Time is the one thing we have plenty of in Cody Town," he said. "And peppermint candy, of course."

"You think this is a joke?"

"No, I don't." His face turned deadly serious, his eyes resonated power. He pointed to the crack in the tiles. Hundreds of insects began crawling through. The soldier toys immediately went to work, stomping on them. "Unless you stop stressing your son out, things are going to get real ugly here."

"Okay," she said. "Fine."

Could Cody be doing this? Was this really some dark recess of his subconscious?

"We both want your son safe and happy," he said. "And another thing. A little gratitude isn't out of the question either."

"Gratitude?"

"If memory serves, Mr. Kevin Stromsky had some terrible things planned for you if I hadn't intervened."

She didn't want to admit it, but he was right. Jarod's transformation *had* provided the perfect cover for her escape. Then when that bastard had tried to kill her in the estate's hallway, Mister Vincent had somehow forced him off her. Probably to stop these cracks from forming in Cody Town. In any case, now wasn't the time to make an enemy here. Not unless it was necessary. And definitely not until her son was in her arms.

"Thank you for saving my life," she said.

"No problem at all," he replied. The toys at the perimeter clapped and clutched their hands over their hearts. Even that crack began to fuse back together. "Now see, there's no reason that this can't be cordial."

Here was her chance.

"I know it wasn't intentional," she said. "But you've unleashed an indestructible monster on us."

"I'm sorry," he replied. "But Jarod doesn't listen too well."

"Tell me how to stop him. Then I promise I'll calm Cody down and leave this place." No way in hell she'd leave her baby behind, but this could be a win-win. Learn how to kill Jarod, while Vincent brought Cody to her. "He must have some weakness."

"It took lifetimes to create that man." He spoke as if Jarod was his prized student. "He has no weakness. Don't worry though. With the way he's burning through the juice that I gave him, he'll be back to his old self soon enough."

"I don't know what that means." She played dumb, though it was obvious that Jarod's transformation was on a timer. When he healed or used his strength, well, that only sped it up. Finally, she had a plan. Wear him down and then put a bullet between his eyes.

"You just have to survive long enough," Mister Vincent said. "Things will settle back to normal."

"Is that all I can do?"

"At this point."

"Okay," she said. "Bring me Cody. He needs his mother."

"Just remember." He smiled, showing teeth with rust stains that hadn't been there before. He lowered his voice, barely above a whisper. "Consequences in Cody Town be damned. If you test me, I'll make sure Jarod eats you in front of your son."

31

Vivian had no doubt that Mister Vincent meant his threat. And yet, standing beside him now, she couldn't calm her nerves. Jarod really could be killed. It wasn't just that, though. Mister Vincent didn't know everything. He was closer to human than she'd thought. Did that mean he could die, too?

Either way, she needed to get Cody and escape this place. Then kill Jarod. Finally, she had a plan.

The front door of the Lego house opened. A teenage boy with a chipped tooth walked out and down the walkway, past a flowerbed of lollipops. He held Cody's hand.

"Don't forget our arrangement," Mister Vincent said. "Calm him, and then I'll send you home safely."

"How do I know that I can trust you?"

"I don't lie," he said as if the idea was beneath him. Then he opened the front picket gate.

"Mommy." Cody pulled away and ran to her.

"I'm here." She ducked down and hugged him close. "Are you hurt?"

He shook his head. "We were playing, but I couldn't find you."

"It's important for a boy to have his mother," Mister Vincent said.

"I love you so much. Mommy will always be here for you."

"Remember." Mister Vincent clicked the gate closed. "It's also important for a mother to know when to let go."

"What is that supposed to mean?" She picked up Cody and stepped back.

"It's okay," Cody told her. "This is Mister Vincent. My friend."

"I know, sweetie." She kissed his forehead and stared at the old man. "What do you want with my son?"

He seemed surprised by her outburst. He surveyed the landscape, apparently searching for more cracks in Cody Town.

"Your boy is quite special," he said calmly, but his eyes seethed as he turned back to her. "You'd be surprised how rare his gift is. He can see both of our worlds. Like his daddy before him."

"Use Jarod then," she said. "Leave us out of this."

"If only I could." A sad look flashed across his face. "It's not in my interest to use someone so young, but Jarod's gift was murdered in a bathtub thirty years ago. What's left of him isn't even a man anymore."

"Have you even tried?"

"What do you think happened last night?" he said loudly, and then seemed to catch himself. "Do you think I enjoyed creating that beast?"

"Why did you do it then?"

"You need to clean out your ears." He pointed a bony finger at her. "I hoped it would work. Instead, it changed him. I've waited thirty years for the Carmichaels to produce a viable offspring. We won't be held back any longer."

Jesus. *We?* Somewhere, there were more Mister Vincents.

"I won't let you turn my baby into a monster."

"Nonsense." He waved the thought away. "His gift isn't broken like his father's. Besides, you don't have much say in the matter, now do you?"

"The hell I don't."

"Keep it up," he said. "And this won't end well."

"Stop scaring Mommy," Cody shouted.

"I wish I could, son." He glared at her. "But just like your daddy, she doesn't listen."

The children moved back from behind the toys. They held hands and formed a giant circle. Their sickly faces whirled by as they began rotating. One way. Then back the other.

"Ring a ring of roses," they chanted. "Sing with us Cody."

"Wait," she told them. "What's going on?"

"It's time," Mister Vincent said. "There's nothing I can do about that."

"What about Cody?" she demanded. "I won't leave him here."

"This will happen. With, or without your blessing."

What could she do? Think. *I don't lie,* Mister Vincent had said. If that were true, then Cody really did have control in this place. What did that mean though? She glanced around, and suddenly she didn't feel so alone.

"Mister Vincent is a bad man, sweetie," she said. "He's scaring Mommy."

Millions of micro-fractures punched the circular clearing. The army of toys chittered and stood at attention. The bear aimed its musket at Mister Vincent's chest.

"Is this how you treat your friends?" There was no mistaking the threat in Mister Vincent's tone. "Who will play with you when Mommy and Daddy won't stop fighting?"

"I will." She held Cody close. "Forever and ever."

"Who will chase away the hand in the closet, or protect you from the Dead Tree?"

Cody looked at her confused. Mister Vincent had been his friend since he could speak. Probably longer. That was nice and all, but she was his mother.

"Mister Vincent wants me to leave you here and never come back," she told Cody.

"No." He shook his head and started crying. Blue electricity arced from Pikachu's back and webbed across the granite.

"Baby." She couldn't control her tears listening to the terror in his voice. "He wants your daddy to kill me."

"Bad Mister Vincent," Cody shouted.

A gunshot echoed across Cody Town. Then two more. The old man stared down at his own chest. Black blood seeped through the three holes in his vest. As he looked up, veins of oil sprang from the corners of his eye.

"I see we're going to have to do this the hard way." He walked toward her. Shadows seeped from cracks in the cobblestone under his feet, leaving puddle footprints of a dark writhing substance.

She held Cody's head against her shoulder, turned, and ran back the way she came. On both sides of the street, giant locusts swarmed from the dead forest, blotting out the florescent sky. Their wings flitted and pecked at her hair and face.

Glancing back, she saw Cody's bear swipe at Mister Vincent with those razor claws. He caught the paw with one hand and tore it off.

She spun back around to find the end of the cobblestone street, where she'd entered Cody Town.

"Can you get us out of here?" she asked.

"I don't know how," he said.

"I won't protect you from Jarod this time." Mister Vincent's voice came from all directions. "What that man's got planned for you—"

The charred forest itself seemed to wake up, devouring the street behind them.

"Get us out of here," Vivian shouted. "Now."

Cody grabbed her face with both of his hands. The colors and lights blinked. Then she felt as though she was squeezed through a tube again. Rain splashed her face. She lay on her side. Cody was still in her arms. They were back on the rooftop in the real world.

"Mommy," he cried.

"I'm here, sweetie." She hugged him. "I love you."

An explosion shook the roof. The helicopter must've crashed. A mushroom cloud of flame and black smoke erupted over the edge of the building, showing Jarod's silhouette fifty feet away. Christ, somehow he'd made it to the rooftop safely.

She got to her feet with Cody in her arms. She'd spent at least fifteen minutes in Cody Town. Here, it seemed that only seconds had passed.

"We should go." Erika ran up to her.

"Take Cody." Vivian handed him over. He began crying. Erika started to protest, so she shouted, "We don't have time to argue. You swore to me that you'd protect him."

Erika considered it, nodded, and then said, "With my life."

She backed away with a struggling Cody in her arms.

"Mommy," he shouted.

"Go," Vivian said. "Before it's too late."

"Butterfly," Jarod called out. She turned to find him walking toward her. "Looks like there's nowhere to left to hide."

She walked over and picked up Officer Franklin's gun from the rooftop. For some reason, she couldn't help but think of her mother and drunken Kenny. Her sister Tammy. Jarod's smirk as he had her arrested that night.

"Good." She turned to face him. "Because I'm through running from you."

rling fit, so she jammed the barrel into his open mouth
d fired until she ran out of bullets. Even through the
tter of gore and guts, the bastard still twitched. His skin
gan to morph.

"Son of a mother-fucking bitch!"

"What are we going to do?" Erika limped over to her.

Vivian staggered to the construction area, found a
ovel for mixing concrete, and then moved back over
od. She placed the tip of the blade on his throat and
mped down on the shovel. Two times. Then three. She
ned down and pried his skull free by his hair.

"Let's see you come back without a fucking head," she
outed.

Erika had a shocked expression.

"What?" Vivian said.

"I didn't say shit."

"Good." She moved to the building's edge and tossed
e head over. A car alarm sounded. Jesus, she could've hit
meone below. She glanced over the side to find the head
bedded in an ambulance's windshield.

"Cody," Vivian said, and then spun to face Erika.

"He's at the nurse's station," she said. "The entire staff
watching him."

"We have to get him."

Vivian hurried back over and checked Jarod's body.
e raised the shovel, ready to leave a limbless torso behind
necessary.

"Is that it?" Erika asked.

32

Rows of lights lined the helicopter's landing pad, yet
the rooftop remained ominously dark. A mixture
of blood and rain dripped down Vivian's arm and
off the end of the gun's barrel. With the wound on her
shoulder and the cuts on her wrist, she felt lightheaded.
Sirens whined, too faint to be useful. It didn't matter,
though. One way or another, this would end tonight.

Yesterday, she'd emptied an entire clip into Jarod's
head, and he'd lived. First, she needed to wear down his
power high. Then she just might be able to kill him. With
her lack of training, she had to get close enough to make
every bullet count.

To the left, Erika carried Cody through the glass access
doors to the hospital. Jarod immediately turned his
attention to them. That didn't make sense. After all this
time, he'd finally gotten her alone. Why not kill her now?

God, it was Cody. Jarod's source of power. Could Mister Vincent give him a reboot? She had no doubt that he could.

"What's the matter?" She limped after him, unwilling to waste bullets yet. "Scared to face me, coward?"

"You'll get your turn." His laughter sounded like screams of pain, but he didn't stop.

"Pretty cocky for someone who's missing an arm," she said.

That got his attention. His neck muscles spasmed as he glared at her.

"I'll gut you where you stand." His large jaw revealed fresh rips in his cheeks. They began healing when he quit talking.

"You might want to check with Mister Vincent first."

"I answer to no one," he roared. "You know nothing."

"I always knew you were a prick," she said. "But sacrificing your own son?"

"He is meat. Nothing more."

She aimed the gun with both hands and fired a test round, which punched his heart. He leapt at her. She rolled to the side. He skidded past her across the wet rooftop and slammed into a pile of construction materials.

For a second, he struggled to free his hook claw from the plastic tarp covering the concrete bags. She fired two more rounds. One missed. How many did that leave? Seven, maybe eight. Was that even enough?

Suddenly, he leapt at her again. Before she could squeeze the trigger, he grabbed her neck with his massive

claw and lifted her off the ground. Snapping th
carried her backward and slammed her into son

With one leg on her chest, he pinned her
along the edge of the building. She swung the g

"Scream for me." He leaned in and dug on
her flesh above her collarbone.

Pain crippled her. She fought with everyth
but a gasp escaped her lips. The gun dropped to

"That's it," he said. "More."

"Fuck you." She tried to shout, but the
without air.

"I like that." His eyes fluttered as he reache
began unbuckling his pants. "I doubt they'll re
when I'm finished."

With her last ounce of strength, she swu
which glanced the side of his head. He sl
released her. No way the blow had that much
kind of spear punched through his chest. Wh
that? Jarod turned around and backhanded
launched five feet. The angled end of a crowbar
his back.

Vivian wrenched it free. Adrenaline surged t
as she slammed him across the head with tl
turned. She struck again, this time with the h
Facial skin tore away, revealing skull and teeth.
Blood poured down his shredded dress shirt, y
began to grow back over his wounds, definitely sl

Quickly, she picked up the gun, shoved it
balls, and fired twice. He dropped to the ro

His body was a ragged mess. No jittering. No healing. No forearm, and his head was down on the street below.

This time there was pretty much no doubt.

"Yes," she said. "It's over."

&ოც

Stromsky sat in the back of the limo, staring at Jarod Carmichael's head embedded in a windshield. He was irritated with the night's events to say the least. His reputation had come into question. Charlotte had even seen fit to commission a second team for a job that he'd been overqualified to handle.

To add insult to injury, Vivian Carmichael, that vile creature, had spit on his suit coat. He dampened his handkerchief with club soda and did his best to clean the filth. Normally he didn't enjoy the unpleasantness of his business. She would be an exception.

His cellular phone rang. He reached into his inner coat pocket and answered.

"Mrs. Carmichael on the line," Charlotte's assistant said. "Please hold."

"Kevin," she said quickly.

"Charlotte, we have important matters to discuss." Normally, manners shouldn't be sacrificed in the interest of time. This wasn't an option tonight. "It seems that a certain group that you've hired has cost us tonight. Their amateurish behavior has set back our objective of secrecy."

"I know, darling. It's terrible."

"I've served the Carmichael family for many years now."

"It was foolish," she said. "I know, but I've always been too anxious when family is concerned. Can you ever forgive an old friend?"

"Water under the bridge, Charlotte. Let us speak of it no more."

"Is there any news?" she asked.

"Your son has been dealt with. After witnessing the night's events, however, I am positive that Vivian needs tending."

"We must do whatever it takes to protect the family. Please call when you're finished, Kevin. We'll meet for tea. We must catch up."

"Until then, Charlotte."

33

Vivian stroked Cody's hair as he slept in the hospital bed. Listening to his tiny snore, she fought the urge to wake him. Could Mister Vincent get to him in his dreams? Maybe, but he'd been through too much tonight. And he couldn't stay awake forever. So she'd keep watch. Every night until the end of time if need be.

Her eyelids felt heavy in the darkness. Though her muscles were already jittery, she reached onto the nightstand, grabbed the bottle of caffeine pills, and washed two more down with her Coke.

As she stood to stretch her legs, her chair squeaked.

"Viv?" Erika's voice sounded groggy. "Is that you?"

"Yeah," she whispered and walked around the hanging blue curtain. Though they were in the musty, abandoned wing of the hospital, she was grateful that Torres had isolated them from the general population.

"What time is it?" Erika blinked and looked down at the IV drip in her wrist.

"Just after five AM. Try to go back to sleep."

"What are you doing up?"

"I got some rest earlier," Vivian said.

For a second, Erika looked around. With her frizzed hair and bandages, she seemed disoriented. Then the don't-bullshit-me look came through her haze.

"When did you find time to sleep?" she asked.

"I'm fine, really." Vivian lied.

Every muscle in her body ached. Her injuries throbbed. The doctor had prescribed pain meds that would cause drowsiness. And they'd stay in her pocket until she was sure Cody was safe.

"Jarod is dead." Erika lowered her voice. "We both saw the body."

"I know." But she wasn't so sure. Could Mister Vincent bring him back? In hindsight, she should've chopped off his other arm and his legs.

"Right now," Erika said. "People are studying what's left of that fool. Do you think they won't notice if he gets up and walks away?"

"It's not just him that I'm worried about."

"Oh." Erika glanced down at her bandaged hand. The memory of Stromsky torturing her best friend made Vivian's stomach turn.

"I'm just being paranoid." She looked around the curtain to double check. Through a small window in the center of the door, she could see Officer Denton eating something.

"How are they acting?" Erika asked.

"Too stupid to know whether to charge me or give me a medal."

"If it makes you feel better, I'll keep watch for a while."

"No, you're a mess." She struggled to find the words, but her mind felt scattered. "Wait, I didn't mean—"

"Look who's talking." Erika pointed at Vivian's bandaged forearm and shoulder. "You're not looking so hot yourself, Giselle."

They laughed. Then harder.

"Okay," Vivian said. "So we're both a mess."

"It's not terrible." Erika held her bandaged hand up and turned it over. "They told me I might get full motion back in my hand once it's healed."

"I'm so sorry."

"Don't." Erika shook her head. "My little man is safe. That's all that matters."

"We wouldn't be alive right now if it wasn't for you." She stopped. How could she convey what she felt? Thank you wasn't enough. Nothing was. "We wouldn't be alive."

"You're not going to make me cry," Erika said. "So you can quit."

They laughed again, quietly this time. She really couldn't remember the last time she'd even smiled.

"By the way," Vivian said. "Your grandma's in the waiting room with Deion."

"She's not going to like this."

"You're safe until morning. They're not allowing visitors."

Cody stirred. She glanced around the curtain. He still slept soundly. Where were the police officers?

"Hold on." She walked to the door. Through the window, she could only see a few feet in each direction. The hallway looked deserted. "I'll be right back. Keep an eye on Cody. If he has a nightmare, wake him."

"What is it?"

"I'll find out." She opened the door and stepped into the dark hallway. "Officer Denton?" she called out.

Nobody answered. She began running to the front desk when the pudgy-faced cop walked out of the men's restroom, drying his glasses with a paper towel.

"Where were you?" she demanded.

"Calm down," he said. "What do you mean?"

Jesus, what was she thinking trusting anyone?

"Please don't leave our room." She began walking back.

"Where's Strauss?" he asked from behind.

"Just do your job."

"He was supposed to stay put." Denton muttered something else under his breath.

She reached the room and walked inside.

"Tomorrow," she said. "Detective Torres needs to find better protection."

Wait, Cody's bed was empty. That's when she noticed the sobbing. She rushed over and pulled back the curtain.

Erika sat with her knees tucked underneath her arms. Tears streamed down her cheeks.

"Where's Cody?" Vivian looked under the bed. Nothing. He couldn't have made it into the hallway in those few moments that she'd gone out there. "Erika. What's going on?"

"It's hideous." She held up her swollen hand. At some point, she'd taken off her bandages. Black stitches lined the fingers that had been reattached. "I'm disgusting."

Were the painkillers affecting her? She'd been fine just a minute before. Vivian pushed the nurse alert button several times.

"Erika, listen to me. Where's Cody?" What if Stromsky had taken him? "Where's my son?"

"I can't do this." She yanked the IV from the top of her wrist and clutched the needle. Blood dripped down her arm.

"Don't." Vivian moved toward her. "The nurses are on the way, honey. Put that down."

"Get away from me," she shouted. "I told you to stay away from that man, but you wouldn't listen."

The door opened behind her. She glanced back to see Officer Denton burst inside.

"What's going on?" he asked.

"My son," Vivian said. "Is he in the hallway?"

"Nobody's out here."

As she turned back, she saw that Erika had made her way over to the window. In those few seconds, she'd managed to open it and climb onto the windowsill. Her hospital gown blew in the wind.

"Oh Jesus, Erika. Come down from there."

"Fuck you," she shouted.

"Please."

"You did this to me. It's all your fault."

"Where my son?" Vivian didn't mean to yell. Immediately, the rage on Erika's face seemed to melt away. She put her head down and began crying again.

"He's not here anymore," she said.

"What?" Vivian's stomach dropped.

Erika looked up. Her lips began quivering. Then she dove out the window. Vivian ran over and tried to grab her, but it was too late. A thud filled her ears as Erika hit concrete.

"Get a doctor," she shouted at the officer. He didn't move. "Go get a doctor."

Suddenly, she saw Cody in the corner. He'd been hiding in the room the entire time, behind a tray of food.

"Baby, cover your eyes," she said to him. Had he been watching this? He began walking forward. "Stay there. Don't look."

Several people ran into the room and shoved Vivian aside.

One of the doctors looked out the window and shouted, "Get paramedics down to the first floor."

"It will be okay," Cody said.

He put his arms around her and helped her up. Then she was in the hallway. She dropped to her knees, hugged him to her chest, and cried. What had changed? Not thirty seconds before, they had just been laughing.

"I warned you what would happen if you tested me," Cody whispered.

"What?" She pulled away and looked into his blue eyes that suddenly seemed harsh.

He wiped tears from her cheek.

"Her blood is on your hands," he said louder this time, in a soft drawl.

Mister Vincent was inside Cody. That monster had taken her son.

III

THE CITY

34

Vivian slammed back against the hallway wall. She struggled to breathe. With his sandy curls and Spiderman t-shirt, Cody looked like himself. Those hateful blue eyes, lined with dark circles, didn't belong to her son though.

"It's time for us to go, Mommy."

"Don't call me that," she snapped at him. "Erika had nothing to do with this."

"I warned you not to be bad."

"You son of a bitch—"

"Better be careful." His tone sounded even more childish. "We don't want them to take me away."

Down the hallway, a group of doctors stared at her. He was right. The police were already on edge. If Child Protective Services stepped in, she'd never get Mister Vincent out of her son.

She grabbed his hand and walked the opposite direction. With every step, she expected some kind of attack, but he moved quietly beside her.

They reached a section of the hospital that had been sealed off for construction. Using moonlight through the plastic-covered windows, she navigated around a paint trolley. Though the power didn't seem to be on here, extension cords ran from down the hallway. She followed them to a hand-held light on the floor.

She hung it from the scaffolding that lined the walls and turned it on. Paint fumes filled her lungs. Almost immediately, her chest tightened further. She pulled out her inhaler and took several puffs.

"Don't lose that again." Eerie shadows crept across Cody's face as the light swayed. "We don't want any accidents."

"I want my son back. You hear me?"

"I told you that I didn't have a choice," he said calmly. "You killed Jarod, so now you don't have a choice either. You're going to take his place and help me finish my work."

"Never."

"I can make it uncomfortable for Cody in here."

In here? Did that mean Cody was trapped back in that sick town? Yes. That had been Mister Vincent's plan all along. Somehow, switching places wouldn't work with Jarod. How could she get back to Cody, though? He'd been the one who'd brought her there the first time. Could he do it again?

"Baby." She leaned down and held his cheek. "If you're in there, come back to me. I love you."

"Don't make me hurt you." He yanked away as if she'd struck him.

She'd hit a nerve.

"Don't listen to anything he tells you," she said. "He's a bad man."

"I'll kill him."

"You can't." She pulled back, paralyzed. "You need him."

"I'll live long after his mind is dead." His giggle gave her chills. "And I won't think twice about leaving you a turnip to care for."

"What do you want from us?" She didn't mean to shout.

"I told you to keep it down."

"What do you want?" she repeated firmly.

"Time to leave," he said. "It's not safe here anymore."

Safe? For her or him? God, Stromsky was still out there.

"The Carmichaels," she said.

"I'd hate for them to kill you before we can finish our work."

She knew he was right, but she wasn't the only one in danger.

"Charlotte tried to have her own son killed," she told him. "What do you think she'll do if you threaten their precious legacy?"

"Good." He smiled. "Now you're getting it. This hospital isn't safe."

"I won't forget what you did to Erika."

"A life for a life." For a brief moment, she saw the same anger on his face that she felt. "There aren't words to describe the punishment for hurting my children, even a damaged one."

"Jarod doesn't make us even. Not by a long shot."

"No," he said. "We're not even, but that doesn't mean anything right now. You want to protect your son, and I need you to travel."

Travel? That sounded so mundane. Almost human. Cody's age really did limit Mister Vincent's plans. But where the hell did he want to go? And to what end? For now, it didn't matter. They needed to leave before the Carmichaels found out that Jarod was dead.

"We'll go," she said. "Just don't pretend that you're him. It makes me sick."

"Fair enough." His face straightened. "Only when it's necessary to keep up appearances." She cringed. Even adult words with Cody's voice sounded perverse. She took his hand.

"Don't talk to anyone on the way out," he said. "Not a word."

He pulled her along the corridor, into the stairway entrance, and then down.

On the first floor, she opened the door to find a deserted lobby. Rubber squeaked to her left. She turned. Detective Torres looked back. Crap. He made eye contact.

"I just heard." His voice echoed off the polished tile floors. "Are you hurt?"

"Don't tell him anything," the voice inside Cody whispered. "Or I'll kill every patient in this hospital."

Torres ran up. For a second, she couldn't speak. Cody squeezed her hand with cold fingers.

"What happened?" Torres asked.

"The window was open." She stopped to hold back her tears. For the last ten minutes, she'd tried to avoid thinking about that moment. Now she couldn't stop the images of Erika lying face down on the concrete. "She jumped."

"Where was Denton? I told that piece of shit not to leave your side."

"It wasn't his fault." She looked down at Cody, furious at the smirk on his face.

"I would've come earlier," Torres said. "But I've been trying to pick up the pieces at the other crime scene."

"It's fine, really."

"I have to talk to you tonight." He looked down at Cody and said quietly, "Alone."

"What about?"

Did he suspect something? He, and a dozen other people, had watched Jarod change into that monster. How long until they figured out that Cody was like his father? She picked him up and tried to hide those eyes with her shoulder.

"One of the nurses can watch him while we talk."

"No," she said. "I won't let them take him."

"After what he's been through, he shouldn't have to hear this."

God, thank you. Torres didn't know anything. Yet.

"Whatever you want to talk about," she said. "It has to wait until tomorrow."

"It can't. The Feds are on their way now."

"I won't let Cody leave my side."

"Fine, but we can't talk out here." Torres motioned into the adjacent room. As she walked inside, she realized that the room was actually a large storage closet for hospital scrubs and other clothing. She turned back to face him.

"We lost more than a dozen officers tonight." He kept his voice low. "You and I need to get some things straight before the FBI arrives."

"What are you talking about?"

"In my twenty-two years on the force, I've never witnessed anything like tonight."

"It was dark," she said. "I didn't see anything."

"Bullshit. You tried to warn me earlier in the orchard, but I wasn't listening. I am now."

"I told you it was dark."

"We both saw your husband change into something...else."

"Let me talk to him, Mommy." Cody tried to pull away, but she held his head firmly against her shoulder.

"No, sweetie. I'll handle this." She looked at Torres. "It's five o'clock in the morning. My son has been through hell tonight, and my best friend is dead."

"I know what I saw," Torres said. "The body on the roof proves it."

"You're crazy," Vivian said. "And if you tell the FBI any of this, I'll make a liar out of you."

"Who do you think they'll believe?" Torres asked. "A wanted fugitive or a decorated officer."

"Run with your story, and we'll see who gets locked in a padded cell."

She moved around him, opened the door, and walked back into the lobby.

"We're not through here," he said from behind.

"There you are." A bald man in glasses rushed straight for the detective.

"I'll speak to you in a moment," Torres told him.

"I warned you people not to use that wing," the man said. "The hospital won't be held accountable for your actions."

This was her chance to get away, but she had no vehicle or money.

"I can't stay in this building anymore." She turned to face Torres. "I need air. Where are you parked?"

"On the curb right out front." He reached into his pocket and grabbed his keys. "Wait there. I'll be out in a second."

Vivian took the keys and walked away. Behind, the two men began arguing. She moved outside and found his Honda double-parked. Then she strapped Cody into the passenger seat. Once in the driver seat, she started the engine. The sky glowed slightly pink as she pulled away.

"Where are we going?" she asked.

"Drive north." He breathed deeply through his nose, as if there were nothing more wonderful than the scent of stale McDonald's.

"North?" That could mean anywhere.

"You might want to hurry." He pointed back at the hospital's sliding glass doors. Her heart skipped. Fifty yards back, Stromsky reached into his front jacket pocket and entered the hospital. "He hasn't seen us yet."

Vivian chirped the tires as she pulled out of the parking lot.

"See, there's no reason that we can't get along," the voice inside Cody said. "I just knew you'd be good at this."

35

A menacing fog rolled over the choppy ocean as Vivian sped across the Bay Bridge. For the last three hours, Cody had remained quiet, except to give directions. With each passing second, the silence grew more terrible.

She had to get that monster out of her son. Did he need a priest? No, Cody Town existed somewhere in his own mind. A psychiatrist?

Yeah, she could see the interaction now. Your son is perfectly fine, Vivian. Don't believe us? Time for some nice Thorazine for your stay in the Cuckoo's nest. What, still not with the program? Here's a quaint Mohawk with matching lobotomy scars.

No thank you.

Still, she couldn't quiet that nagging voice that told her that Mister Vincent wasn't a demon or a ghost. That he existed in some bitter wasteland beyond the reach of modern science. Not that it mattered. It wasn't as though she worked for NASA.

At least the clergy were trained to consider things beyond our understanding, weren't they? Back in Cody Town, Mister Vincent seemed old. If that were true, the Roman Catholic Church must've come into contact with him, or something like him before.

So a priest was her best shot, but she couldn't exactly take Cody to a cathedral while he watched her every move. For now, she had to play along and wait for her break. Ahead, San Francisco's skyline disappeared into the fog.

"We're in the city now," she said. "Which exit should I take?"

He didn't respond. She looked over and found him leaned against the door, sound asleep. Finally. Her chance. Could Mister Vincent see her now? No, or else he would've awakened to direct her.

More than ever, she was convinced. Cody wasn't just a gateway for Mister Vincent. He was also a prison. The bastard was trapped inside a four-year-old. That's why he didn't want to use *someone so young*. Why she wasn't dead yet. He needed her to protect him.

Where was the closest cathedral? St. Patrick's Church, she knew, off Mission Street. Calmly, she drove, until they reached the Fourth Street exit. She slowed onto the off ramp.

"What are you doing?" He sat up in his seat.

This wasn't going to work. Cody had always been a light sleeper. How could she get him to stay out long enough to talk to a priest?

"I asked you a question," he said.

The sleeping pills that the nurse had given her. They were still in her pocket. He wouldn't just take them though. She'd have to hide them with food.

"I'm starving," she told him. "We have to eat."

"Get back on the highway."

"I have to stretch my legs." She spotted the Bay Street Diner and pulled into the parking lot. "We won't be that long."

"You must like to hurt your son."

"Dammit." She slammed on the brakes and held him against the seat. "I need coffee and food. If I fall asleep at the wheel, we'll crash."

An elderly couple stopped crossing the parking lot and stared. Her window was rolled down.

"Sorry," she told him. If she was going to save her baby, she couldn't afford to lose control. "I'm hungry and I haven't slept. I need coffee to stay awake."

He seemed to consider it. Finally, he said, "We'll eat."

"Thank you."

"You should know." He unclicked his seatbelt. "I've built pyramids and murdered kings. Nothing you're considering is going to work."

Jesus, did he know that she was planning to drug him? No, or else he would've taken the pills from her. They got out of the car. Cody walked around to her.

"Fix yourself up," he said.

She looked down. Great. The last thing they needed was to draw attention. Her sweater was ripped, and she was bandaged to all hell. At least the dried blood on her jeans looked like paint stains. She opened the Honda's door, pulled Torres's puffy Dodgers jacket from the backseat, and put it on. Cody nodded and held out his hand. She took it.

As they walked inside, the scent of spattered grease and onions filled the room. A young waitress turned from the grill.

"Seat yourselves anywhere," she said.

With Cody walking in front, Vivian took two pills from her pocket and palmed them. They sat in a window booth.

The waitress walked up, pulled a pen from behind her ear, and looked down at Cody.

"Hey cutie pie. Aren't you just the sweetest thing?"

"Hamburger," he said. "Bloody rare."

"Okay." She laughed nervously. "And what to drink?"

"Black coffee."

That was how Vivian could slip him the pills. The heat would dissolve them. How many though? Given his size and lack of sleep, one should be more than enough.

The server gave her a look, and she realized how crazy his food order sounded from a four-year old.

"He has a condition," Vivian told her. "The caffeine helps."

"Oh."

"The same for me," she told her. "But well done."

The waitress dotted her notepad and seemed relieved to walk away.

"Get the check when she comes back," he said. "I don't want to be late."

"What are we doing here?" she asked. He just stared at her. "We're in San Francisco already. I'm going to know soon enough."

"Last time I checked, Charlotte Carmichael had reservations at a spa retreat." An evil smile crossed his face. "I've owed her a visit for many years now."

"Are you nuts? Stromsky works for the family. They'll kill us on sight."

"Don't you worry. I've got something special planned for Mr. Kevin Stromsky."

All morning, she'd wondered why Mister Vincent hadn't unleashed whatever hell he had planned. Everything made sense now. He had enemies that knew at least part of his secret, and he couldn't begin until he dealt with them. The minute they were out of the picture, it would start. Vivian had to stop that meeting.

"You're going to get my son killed," she whispered.

"You just do your part, and I'll give him back in one piece."

"I want to talk to him," she said.

"You'll see him when our work is finished."

"Either let me talk to my son, or—"

"You'll do what?" He moved his silverware to the side, took his napkin from the table, and placed it in his lap. "I'd hate to have to punish the boy for your actions."

"Just tell me where he is." Her voice choked up. "Is he safe?"

"He's fine. Playing with others like himself as we speak."

"In Cody Town?" She quieted her voice. "With those diseased kids?"

"Believe me." He smiled. "They'll take good care of him in my absence."

The server walked up with their drinks, and he stopped talking.

"Careful, honey." She set down the mugs and also two waters. "It's hot."

Vivian reached for her cup and deliberately knocked over a water glass.

"Dammit," she said.

"It's no big deal. I'll grab a towel." The waitress walked away.

Ice water began dripping into his lap, but he just stared at her with those cold eyes. Did he suspect something?

"Are you just going to sit there?" she asked.

The doorbell chimed and two cops walked in. Here was her distraction.

"The police are here," she said quietly.

He turned around, and she dropped the pill into his coffee.

"They're just here to eat." Cody turned back to her. "Don't make a scene."

The cops walked in the opposite direction and sat down. The server returned with the towel and dried the table.

Cody blew on the mug and swallowed it down. What if the pills didn't dissolve? God, what if he noticed the taste? They sat in silence until the food arrived. As they ate, he drank more, and his eyes seemed to get heavier. It was working.

"Is there anything else I can get for you two?" The server asked.

"Just the check," Vivian said.

In her peripheral view, she saw him slump over, and fall asleep in the seat.

"Oh how cute." The server set the bill on the table. "He's zonked out."

"He's had a long day."

Vivian's stomach turned as she paid the bill. How long would those pills last? At least three hours. It wasn't much. And when he woke, he'd know what she'd done. She carried Cody out to the car. Three hours to find out what Mister Vincent was. Three hours to save her baby.

∽✺∾

Everything in Cody Town was covered in mud now, even here inside his Lego House. Cody scrunched into a ball behind the bookcase. Every night when they were hiding from Daddy at the cabin, he came here when he went to sleep. Now he couldn't stop crying. Nothing was the same. Not since Mister Vincent got mad at him. Now it was dark and wet. Bear and his toys were dead. He wanted to leave, but he didn't know how to wake up anymore.

Sometimes, Mommy called his name from far away, but when he tried to go to her, the bigger kids stopped him. Maybe if he hid long enough, they would forget about him. Then he would run away and never come back.

"Cody." Little Girl walked inside. Her yellow Alice-in-Wonderland dress still looked brand new from the store. "Come outside, silly."

"Go away," he said, but he really didn't mind her.

Even though she forgot her name like the other kids, Little Girl was the nicest one. At least she moved her lips when she talked.

"Why do you stay in here?" she asked. "There's not even a roof anymore."

"I don't care." Most of the walls of his house were gone too, but he still felt safer inside.

"Come play with us."

"No." He looked up at the sky. A million-billion wings buzzed. Giant bugs flew everywhere. They looked like moving thunderclouds.

"What's the matter?" she asked. "Frightened of the bone pinchers?"

"I'm not scared," he told her.

One of the bugs landed on top of the crooked wall and chewed off another piece of his plastic house.

"Get out." Cody threw a Matchbox car at it. The bug flapped its wings at him and chomped its teeth. The see-through skin on its chest began clicking and its insides lit up.

"They're beautiful." Little Girl grabbed his hand and shoved it down. "They never harm us if we behave."

"Make it go away."

"If you promise to play with us."

He nodded.

"*Bone pincher, bone pincher,*" she sang. "*Go find your home, feed on the others, and leave us alone.*"

The bug's belly calmed down. It tilted its head and rubbed its front arms over its mouth. Finally, it flew away.

"Just remember the song." She sat Indian-style next to him. "It's the only thing that calms them."

He hugged her. From here, the black bump on the side of her neck looked bigger. It had freckles, too.

"Does it hurt?" He touched it, super gentle.

"Not anymore, silly." She giggled. "When you stay here long enough, nothing hurts anymore."

He didn't know why, but he really missed Mommy right then. And Auntie Erika. And Daddy, but only when he wasn't bad.

"Now come outside," she said. "We're playing your favorite game. Bloody Shoe."

"I don't want to."

"You promised us." She looked meaner. "Do you know what happens when you break promises here?"

"I don't care." He moved farther into the corner. "Leave me alone."

Little Girl stayed quiet for a second. Then she looked down at her dress and picked a lint ball from it.

"Cody, if I tell you something about your mom, can you promise to keep it secret?"

"Did you see her?" He leaned closer.

"Maybe."

"Where?"

"Criss-cross, promise not to tell." She made an X over her chest, so he did, too. "I met her when she came to Cody Town before. We laughed and laughed. Horsey was there, too." She reached out and held his hand. "She told me that you were such a bad boy that she didn't love you anymore."

"You're lying," he shouted.

"Shhh." Little Girl peeked through the broken window at the other kids. "You don't want to anger them. They do things sometimes."

"She loves me." He tried not to cry.

"Cody, once you get used to it here, you'll be so happy. We can be your family now. Forever and ever."

"Mommy loves me. She's coming to get me."

"Where is she?" Little Girl looked around the room. "I don't see her."

"She doesn't know how to get here. I'll tell her."

"You don't even know where she is."

"Yes, huh." He pointed where he heard her voice sometimes. Far away, toward the big dead tree. It looked darker down there. And colder.

"You really are a bad boy." She stood up.

"Cody, Cody." The twin boys, whose tummies were stuck together, crawled inside the house. They had no legs, so they always walked like a backwards spider. The rest of the kids followed behind. Cody hid behind Little Girl.

"Where are you going, Cody?" they asked. Their lips and faces didn't move.

"Cody wants to leave us." Little Girl pushed him away. "He wants to go past the Dead Tree."

"I'm going home," he shouted at them.

"No, no, no." They sounded mad.

"They're right," Little Girl said. "Who's going to play with us?"

"Play with us," the other kids chanted. "Play with us."

"I tried to warn you." Little Girl smiled at him. Two bone pinchers landed on his broken bookshelf with their stomachs lit up. Then three.

"Play with us. Play with us."

He didn't know what to do. They would never let him leave. Then he remembered that time underneath the cantaloupes in the grocery store, when Mommy yelled at him because she had to get the manager to find him.

"I hate Bloody Shoe," he told them. "Let's play Hide-and-seek."

"Perfect." Little Girl laughed. "Cody should be it. You are the best."

"No," he said. "You all count to ten and I hide."

"You're so clever," Little Girl said. "All of us are it."

"No peeking."

They turned away from him. Even Little Girl covered her eyes.

"One," she said. "Two."

Cody ran outside to the front gate, opened it quietly, and stared at the Dead Tree in the distance. All kinds of bugs crawled from cracks in the road. The sky was filled with bone pinchers, but Mommy loved him and missed him. He knew she did. He had to find her.

36

Vivian screeched to a stop across the street from Saint Patrick's Church. Two teenagers jumped back. She checked the clock. Eleven-forty-three a.m. She'd already wasted fifteen minutes in traffic just getting here.

She lifted Cody from the passenger seat into her lap. Though she'd only given him one pill, his body seemed too limp. Had it been too much? What if it wasn't enough?

"Don't worry." She held his head against her shoulder and exited the car. "I promise, I'll fix it."

All around, skyscrapers loomed over the church. A chilled, salty-ocean wind stung her cheeks as she crossed the street and entered the building.

Inside, the cathedral's one massive hall, its round columns and stained glass windows—even its pipe organ—reached a height of four stories. The sounds of city traffic beyond the walls disappeared, leaving an uncomfortable quiet.

Although there was no service, scattered parishioners sat in the pews. She raced down the center aisle. At the front, an Asian custodian used a thirty-foot pole to hang a flag above the granite altar.

"I need to speak with the head priest," she said, unsure if that's what he was called.

"He's busy right now," the man said in broken English. "Come back later."

She opened the brass gate that separated the altar from the congregation and moved inside.

"You can't come in here," he said.

"I have to see the person in charge."

"It's okay, Hugh," a voice called out to her left.

She turned. A forty-something man with short gray hair came out of a bordering room. He wore a standard black button up shirt with a Roman collar.

"I'm Father Adrian," he said. "We're going to start Mass soon, but you can stop by after if you'd like to discuss—"

"I need your help now," she said. "My son's possessed."

"Okay." He nodded slowly. Had it been a mistake to come here? No. This was her only chance to save Cody. She couldn't blow it. "Please, just listen to what I have to say."

Somebody coughed behind her. She turned to find a family gawking at them. The daughter held up her cell phone. Was she filming this? Vivian realized how she looked in her bloody jeans.

"Let's step into the sacristy," Father Adrian said.

She followed him into the room from which he'd just come. Gold chalices, robes, and books were stacked on a shelf against the far wall. He closed the door behind them and turned on a desk lamp.

"There isn't much time," she said. "I need to know if you can help us."

"Tell me what's going on."

She closed her eyes and took a deep breath. At least he was listening.

"My son isn't himself anymore," she said. "Something has taken his body. I thought all this time he was talking to an imaginary friend, but it's not. And now it's taken control of him."

"I have to ask." He folded his arms. "Have you had anything to drink today? Any medication?"

"I'm sober, and I'm not crazy."

"Okay. When did you first see this change in him?"

"Last night."

"And where is his father?"

"What does that have to do with anything?" she asked.

"Please don't take offense. Sometimes children from broken homes act out in strange ways."

Cody stirred, and she froze. Was he waking up? She couldn't let that happen here. At least if they were still on the road, she could pretend that they hadn't strayed from the plan. He settled back down.

"Listen, either you can help me," she said. "Or I have to go."

"No, please stay. I'm listening. Just let me look at him."

She gently moved Cody from her shoulder and cradled him in her arms.

"Something's wrong." Father Adrian put his hand over Cody's forehead.

"What do you think I've been trying to tell you?"

"No." He hurried over and picked up his phone from the desk. "He looks really sick. We have to get him to a doctor."

"We can't." She looked down at Cody's ghost pale skin. At the curls clinging to his forehead. "We have to get this thing out of him first."

"Listen to me. Demons don't exist." He punched in some numbers. "Nobody sleeps like that. When was the last time he's eaten?"

"You don't understand," she said. "I gave him a pill so he could sleep."

"Excuse me." He glared at her. "What did you give him?"

Her chest felt empty. This was her last option. Her only chance to stop Mister Vincent.

"What did you give him?" Father Adrian demanded.

"I'm sorry." She took a step back. "But there's nothing you can do for us."

"No. Wait." He moved over to her. "We can help him."

"Any moment now, my son will wake up. God help us then."

"Don't say that, Mommy." Cody stared up at her. She nearly dropped him. "You've been telling our secrets."

"No." She shook her head. "I haven't said a word."

"You know I can't let him leave now." He reached out and grasped the man's hand. Father Adrian recoiled, as if in pain.

"A church, Vivian?" Cody appeared oblivious to the priest now. "That was your great plan?"

Was this it? Would she end up like Erika? She grabbed his cheeks.

"I know that you're in there, baby," she said. "I love you."

"If you don't put me down now, I'll tear Cody Town from your son. I'll leave him to be devoured."

She immediately set him on the floor, and his legs wobbled. The drugs were still working.

"Please don't hurt him," she said.

"I'll deal with you later."

A loud clatter. Then the lights dimmed. She looked up to see Father Adrian knock a lamp from the desk. Shadows rolled across the walls as the priest clutched his hands to his head. Seconds later, he raced past them into the main hallway.

"We'd better go." Cody held out his hand. "I think that man's a cutter."

"What?" she asked. "What are you talking about?"

A woman's scream echoed into the room. Seconds later, a man's yell chilled Vivian's blood. It was beginning.

34

Vivian ran out of the sacristy to the altar. Dozens of screaming people bottlenecked at the front door. In the commotion, she couldn't see Father Adrian. Every chandelier shut off at once. She looked down at Cody.

"What did you do to him?" she demanded.

"You might want to keep it down." His eyes seemed to shine in the darkness. "They won't attack me once they've turned, but you're a bright little flower, aren't you?"

"Shut up." She couldn't take that voice coming from her baby anymore. "Just shut your mouth."

"I'm not the one who needs to quit drawing attention to themselves."

"Please don't," a woman yelled in the main hall, followed by a cry of pain that was cut short.

She picked up Cody and crept across the carpet. Dim light filtered through rows of stained-glass windows above. A squishing noise filled her ears as she stepped.

"Careful." Cody pointed down.

The custodian lay on the floor in a pool of blood, clutching his neck. He stopped shaking. Then his muscles relaxed.

Directly ahead, the exit seemed miles away. Parishioners rushed outside, until she couldn't see anyone else in the church. She stepped around the corpse, and then over to the brass gate.

Maybe fifty feet down the center aisle, a man knelt between her and the light of the front door. It had to be the priest. He hummed over the sounds of ripping cloth.

"Move slowly," the voice inside Cody whispered. "He might not even notice you."

She gently opened the gate to the altar. Just as she stepped through, it slipped from her sweaty fingers. The metal bars clanged shut.

Father Adrian spun and faced her. Beside him, she could barely see a woman lying on her back.

"There you are." He sat poised. "Come here. I've found the problem."

"You'd better talk to him," the voice inside Cody said. "You don't want to rile that man."

"What problem did you find?" She tried to sound calm.

"I can save these people. I can finally save them."

"I don't know what you mean," she said.

"Come here. I'll show you."

His reached inside the stomach cavity of the woman lying beside him and began a sawing motion.

"She's still alive," she told Cody. "Stop this. I'll take you anywhere."

"It's beyond anyone's control now," he said. "Even mine."

"I always knew that men were flawed by design," Father Adrian said over his shoulder. "But I never understood why." He yanked a handful of flesh free from the woman. Her muffled scream sounded as if the air had been stolen from her lungs. "It's this organ right here that's the problem. All this time, it's been in front of me."

Vivian darted along the first pew.

"Where are you going?" he shouted from behind.

The aisle ended with a huge crucifix. She turned right. A loud thumping sound gained on them. Glancing back, she saw the priest leap over seats to get to her.

"You're not clean," he shouted. "Don't you go outside."

She reached the back wall just as the man cleared the last bench. He landed between her and the door. His deep breaths sounded angry.

"Please just listen to me." She set Cody on the floor.

"I need to fix these people." He pointed a sharp object at her. "Where do you think you're going?"

"I'm here to help you." She struggled to catch her breath. "That's all."

"Why did you run?" he demanded.

"I just wanted to find people for you to fix."

For a second, he studied her.

"That's good thinking," he said as if nothing had happened. "It's too big a task for one man. Of course, you know I'm going to have to clean you first."

"Not yet." She stepped back.

He lunged at her and snatched her shirt. Shadows whirled around. Her head smacked the carpet. She looked up to find him sitting on top of her. He pulled up her shirt, exposing her stomach.

"I didn't want this." Cody stood over her. The priest seemed oblivious to him. "Don't say I didn't warn you."

"This might sting a bit." The man brought the knife down.

"Stop," she shouted. "You're making a mistake."

"What?"

"Not yet…" What could she say? "You can't fix me yet."

"What are you talking about?" he asked with an earnest look on his face.

"You can't fix me because you're still broken," she said.

"Jesus Christ our savior has allowed me to see. He will guide my hand."

"You're wrong. You're just like the rest of us." She pointed to his chest. "Look."

He lifted his shirt.

"My God." He removed his glasses and wiped his forehead with his sleeve. "We're going to have to take care of this right now."

He stood and helped her up.

"Not bad." Cody began clapping.

"I might need your help to get all of it." Father Adrian unbuttoned his shirt. "I don't want it growing back."

"I'll make sure." Her heart pounded. They walked to the center aisle, and he sat down.

In the candlelight, she could see the blade in his hand was a box cutter. He began carving into his own stomach, and she turned away.

Jarod had been a bastard from the start, but this man had been decent. It had only taken one touch from Mister Vincent to drive him insane. Erika, too.

The priest moaned. In her peripheral view, she could see him wrestling deeper and deeper into his own stomach until he finally slumped over. She turned to Cody.

"Why are you doing this?" she asked.

"Your kind has been alone, unsupervised for too long now, like a festering sore," he said matter-of-factly. "I've got to clean the infection before I can make way for the others."

"You want to kill everyone?" She didn't even see how that was possible, even for him.

"Don't you worry," he said. "I'm sure that we'll find some use for you. Maybe a handful of others."

"A use?" She stood in a daze. She couldn't believe what she was hearing.

"We'd better go now." Cody held out his hand. She pulled hers back.

"I choose who to turn, and I like you firing on all six." He walked over to her and forced her to take his hand.

The front doors to the church sat wide open. Nothing stood between Mister Vincent and that meeting now. When he was finished with Jarod's family, he'd unleash his hell on San Francisco. Then what? New York. Then Tokyo? No matter what, she couldn't let that happen. Tears filled her eyes as she thought of what that might mean.

38

Vivian walked down the front steps of St. Patrick's Church. Beams of sunlight carried the scent of churros. She glanced down at the thing pretending to be her son and shivered. One touch. That's all it had taken for Mister Vincent to murder four people. Father Adrian's heavy breathing as he cut that woman open...as he cut into himself. Erika's ranting just before she jumped from the hospital window.

Cody needed to be isolated from the population. At least until she could figure out a way to remove Mister Vincent. How could she get him out of the city though? The car's trunk. It was the only way to make sure that he didn't touch her. The thought of locking her baby in cramped darkness sickened her. No, it wasn't Cody. Not anymore. And it had to be done. Once they got back to Torres's car, she'd make her move.

Directly ahead, Cody stepped off the curb into the road. She leapt forward and yanked him back. A Harley roared by.

"What are you doing?" she shouted. "You're going to get my son killed."

"Take me over there." He pointed across the street.

Looking up, she saw an elderly woman crying in the arms of a teenager. A crowd formed around them. Some of the people talked on cell phones. Other survivors of Father Adrian's attack waved at her and Cody to come across the street with them.

"Haven't you done enough?" she asked.

In the distance, a live music band began playing. Cheers and laughter wavered in and out on the wind. Behind the group of parishioners, a red haired girl chased a balloon over a grassy hill. Beyond that, the city park seemed to be filled to capacity with families.

"My date with Charlotte has been put on hold." Cody looked up at her. "It's time we got started."

"We can't." Somehow, she had to get him back to Torres's car. "Stromsky's still out there. If you start now, he'll know where to find us."

"Mr. Kevin Stromsky killed forty-three people in his entire life. You'll have to forgive me if I'm not impressed."

"What about the police? They'll be here soon."

"Whose fault is that?" he snapped at her. "You've tipped my hand. Charlotte will be expecting me now. If Mr. Stromsky kills your boy, at least you'll know who to blame."

"No." Her voice quivered. "You won't let that happen."

"No, I won't, if you do as you're told." He reached for her hand. "This is your last chance."

This was it. That monster wasn't going to use her baby anymore. She snatched his long sleeves, careful to avoid his hands.

"Get off me." He gritted his teeth. For a second, she could almost see Mister Vincent's true face. "Last warning."

"I won't let you do this," she said.

Brakes squealed. She looked up as a police car stopped beside them. The crowd of parishioners swarmed around it. If they arrested her now, nothing would stand in Mister Vincent's way. She clamped his wrists together with one hand, picked him up around his waist, and hurried down the sidewalk. A car door slammed behind her.

"Help me," the voice inside Cody screeched. "She's a stranger."

"Wait," a man shouted from behind. She dodged pedestrians and picked up her pace. "The woman carrying the child, I said hold up."

Vivian glanced back. A squat, barrel-chested officer raced down the sidewalk after her. People jumped from his path. There was no way to outrun him like this. She turned to face him. His hand rested on what looked like a Taser gun in his belt.

"Don't you aim that thing near my son." She stepped back.

"Quit running," he said. "I just want to talk."

All around, people parted from them.

"She's a stranger." Cody struggled in her arms.

"Put the child down. Get on the ground."

"You don't understand," she said. "He's autistic."

"Now." The officer pulled out his Taser.

Cody yanked his arm free and reached for her face. She dropped him. Immediately, he darted into traffic. Tires shrieked. An SUV slid just short of him. She raced across the street after him. The officer grabbed her sweater and yanked her back. She struggled to break free, but he bear-hugged her.

"What the hell's going on?" A female officer ran up.

"I've got this," he said. "Just grab the kid. He's right there."

"No." Vivian looked at her. "Don't touch him. He's infected with something."

"Shut up." A rough hand pinched her neck, shoved her over to the sidewalk, and forced her down to the ground. "Don't struggle. It will only make this worse."

"Listen to me," she shouted with her face against the concrete. The female officer approached Cody. "Whatever you do, don't touch him."

"I said shut your mouth." The man on Vivian's back yanked her arm. Pain exploded in her shoulder. The rattle of a steel cuff bit into her wrist.

From the corner of her eye, she saw the female officer approach Cody. They were maybe ten feet way.

"Please help me find my real Mommy." He looked back at Vivian. The son of a bitch winked, and then turned back to the officer. "I miss her."

Then he touched the woman's wrist. She jerked her hand back.

"Dammit," Vivian shouted at the man on her back. "It's starting. We have to stop him."

The monster pretending to be her son looked at her. He touched a man who stood next to the female officer. Then a teenage girl behind him. And another. And another. Again, until he disappeared into the crowded park.

৩৩৩

Cody was terrified of the muddy road he walked down. Above, bone pinchers flew and chewed and clicked their teeth, but they didn't try to eat him. Was he going the right way? Mommy's voice always came from down here, but he hadn't heard her since he left. She had to be here somewhere.

"Dammit." Mommy's voice sounded like it came from everywhere. "It's starting. We have to stop him."

"Don't leave me here," he shouted. "I want to go home."

"Cody," somebody whispered next to him. "Don't leave us."

He spun around. A bone pincher flew in front of his eyes. For a second, he saw a flash of yellow on the side of

the road. Little Girl's Dress. Cody turned and ran for the
Dead Tree.

39

The crowd in the park began to throb. With her chin mashed to the sidewalk, Vivian struggled to break free of the officer on her back. Somehow, she had to make this cop understand the danger that the city was in.

"Listen to me." Her lungs felt crushed under his weight. "I have to get to get my son. He's sick."

"Save it." He released her and grabbed her free wrist. "If you're telling the truth, they'll sort it out down at the station."

"It'll be too late, then."

Ten feet away, his partner dropped to her knees. One after another, members of the crowd fell as well. She couldn't see Cody anywhere.

"My son is sick," she shouted at him. "All of these people are in danger."

"Jenson is getting him now."

"Are you blind?" Vivian shouted. "Look."

His partner grabbed handfuls of her own hair. She yanked downward until strands tore free. Several gasps came from the crowd. Others cheered. Too many others. It had been less than thirty seconds. How many of these people had Mister Vincent infected?

"What the fuck." The officer on her back stood. He handcuffed Vivian to a park bench's iron frame. She could finally breathe again. "Jenson," he yelled at his partner. "What are you doing?"

"You're not listening," Vivian said. "If we don't find my son, this is going to get worse."

A biker in a leather jacket stepped from the crowd. She'd seen Cody touch that man a few moments before.

"Get up you pig fuck," he shouted at the female officer, who remained on her knees with a confused look on her face.

The biker threw what looked like an unopened soda can. It smacked her eyebrow, dropped to the sidewalk, and hissed as it sprayed out. Blood poured down her face and over her lips, but she didn't cry out or even react. Instead, she tried to hand him the tufts of her own hair as he approached.

"Freeze motherfucker." The officer next to Vivian pulled his weapon. Calmly, the biker took Jenson's gun from her belt. "Don't fucking move or—"

The biker shot her in the face. Her body flung backward. Gunshots and screaming everywhere. Vivian kicked to the edge of the sidewalk to avoid the stampeding crowd. More gunfire. Glancing back, she saw the officer chase after the killer down the street.

A heavyset woman looked directly at Vivian. She held a hand over her mouth as if to control a giggle. Then she stepped into traffic. A Cal-Trans work truck didn't have time to brake. It smacked her. Instantly, she folded under the grill. The truck bounced over her body and screeched to a halt.

Hundreds of voices began crying and shrieking, but the laughter was worst of all. And her baby was out there somewhere.

She pulled on her handcuffs, but it was useless. The police would lock her up on sight. Detective Torres might not though. He *had* seen Jarod change. And he might be able to reason with San Francisco PD.

To her left, an elderly woman pulled out a lighter and hobbled to the middle of the street. She began burning the body of the woman under the truck.

Vivian crawled behind a trashcan. She managed to pull her cell phone from her back pocket. Careful not to draw any attention, she dialed Torres's number.

He answered on the first ring. "Where are you?"

"San Francisco," she said quietly. "Mission Street. Across from Saint Patrick's Church. Please, I need you to send somebody to help me."

"I'll be there in five minutes."

"You're in San Francisco already?" That didn't make sense. When she'd left him, they'd been in Santa Barbara. Had he been following her?

"Five minutes." He hung up.

ʚϹϹɞ

All around Vivian, the people had thinned out. Traffic had stopped completely. The car's drivers were all gone. From where she hid, only four bodies were in view, but she could hear screaming everywhere. Torres needed to hurry. The building's shadows had grown longer. It would be night soon.

Finally, he raced from the park with his gun drawn.

"Thank God." With her arm cuffed, she awkwardly tried to stand.

"You're real damn lucky that my car has Lo-Jack."

"We have to get Cody. He's out there."

"Shut up." He unlocked her cuff and pulled her to the police car still parked in the street. "You knew this was going to happen. I saw it on your face this morning."

"Cody just went through the park. We've got to find him."

"I just came through. He's not there."

"Please, just listen—"

"No," he said. "You sold your last goddamn wolf ticket when you stole my car this morning."

"I ran from you because you were in danger."

"I was in danger," he said. "Right."

"I couldn't talk. If you knew too much, you'd be dead right now."

"Have you even seen what's going on out there?" he shouted. "It's a fucking nightmare. You knew this was coming, and you didn't even warn these people."

His words stopped her. He was right. There were no excuses.

"It's almost dark." She fought back her tears. No matter how she'd failed him, Cody was innocent and good. He didn't deserve to be left with Mister Vincent's diseased children. "My baby's out there. He's all alone."

Torres stared into the park for a second. Somebody screeched over the chorus of car alarms. The voice didn't even sound human.

"I'll put out an Amber Alert," he finally said. "But in this mess, I'm not making any promises."

"No." She shook her head. "We have to find him ourselves."

"You're not making sense." He leaned into the car's window and grabbed the radio. "We'll have the entire city searching for him."

What could she tell him? If he knew what Cody was, would he want to kill him? No. Through all of this, Torres had been pigheaded and rude, but he was a good man. And if she hoped to stop Mister Vincent, she'd need his help.

"We have to isolate Cody," she said. "If you send those officers after him without warning them, they could get hurt."

"Come again?" He lowered the radio.

"You saw Jarod last night."

"Are you telling me that Cody is responsible for this?"

"Something is inside of him."

"What is it?"

"He calls himself Mister Vincent," she said. "He's driving these people insane. All it takes is one touch."

"I promise you." He pointed in her face. "You're going to answer for this."

"Fine, send me away forever," she said. "Just help me stop this."

"We have to quarantine him."

For once, they agreed.

Where would Mister Vincent go? Somewhere he could inflict the most damage. Fisherman's Wharf? Golden Gate Park? The list of targets in the City was endless.

"Radio to dispatch," he said into the CB. "I need an Amber Alert and a possible CDC quarantine on a four year old boy last seen on Mission Street." He looked at Vivian. "Is he still wearing the same clothes?"

"Yes."

"Spiderman shirt, jeans, and blue Nikes," he told dispatch.

"Hold on," the radio voice said. For a long moment, silence. "Did you say he's wearing a Spidey shirt?"

Torres looked at her for verification. She nodded.

"Yeah," he said.

"After the day we've had, finally some good news."

"What do you mean?" Torres asked.

"Your kid," the dispatcher said. "I think he just walked through the front doors."

ɛ◝ɛ◝

Stromsky's limo had almost reached Mission Street when his cell phone vibrated. On the television, a ten second loop of Vivian and young Cody Carmichael played on CNN. They were standing in Saint Patrick's Church. On the closed captioning, the anchor was describing the church's priest as patient zero. What a mess. Technology made secrecy in his job nearly impossible these days. Still, the situation wasn't beyond cleaning.

His phone buzzed again. He reached into his inner coat pocket and answered.

"Mrs. Carmichael on the line," her assistant said. "Please hold."

"Have you been watching the news?" she immediately said.

"I assure you, Charlotte, the situation is under control. I'll be at the church shortly."

"That won't be necessary," she said. "I'm cutting off any ties from that side of the family."

Clean the entire family before they can cause more damage to the Carmichael name. Cody included.

"I understand," he said.

"I don't think that you do." Her voice carried a steely edge. "I've already sent two reporters from my doorstep tonight. Your services are no longer required."

"I've protected the Carmichael family for many years now. Have I failed you yet? In twenty-four hours, this will be just a bad—"

"What you do is your own business, Mr. Stromsky," she said. "Good day."

She hung up.

40

Vivian explained as much as she understood to Torres, who sped down a cramped, one-way street with sirens blaring. Ahead, cars barely had room to pull over for them, making it almost impossible to navigate the hilly street. When she finished, he picked up the police radio.

"This is Detective Torres," he said. Only static crackled. "Is anyone listening?"

No answer. In less than ten minutes, all contact with the station had gone silent.

"How long until we get there?" she asked.

"It's not far, but we have to assume he won't stay put. Where would this Mister Vincent try to go next?"

"Somewhere with lots of people," she said.

"That can be anywhere." Torres took a right. The tires chirped. "Think. He must have said something."

"Only that he thinks that we're an infection. He wants to clean us off the earth."

"What, humans?" Torres asked sarcastically.

"I think that's what he meant."

"He's four-years old, and he's on foot. Mister Vincent or not, how much damage could he possibly inflict?"

"I don't know, but look around. You saw what happened to Jarod last night."

"Even if he takes out every precinct, shit, if by some miracle he touches every person in this city, the National Guard will step in and they'll have the firepower—"

"Oh my God," she said.

"What?"

It all made sense now. Why Mister Vincent wasted no time getting to the police. He was working his way up to the armed forces. Lunatics with assault weapons. Tanks. Helicopters. Maybe worse.

"What happens when the police department fails?" she asked. "How long until the military arrives?"

"They'd have to declare a state of emergency first." Torres slammed the brakes and screeched left. "Oh Fuck."

The seatbelt dug into her chest and snapped her back. The cab of the police car grew warm.

Ahead, the power was out. Towers of flame poured from storefronts as far as she could see. Hundreds of people raced through grid-locked traffic. A mother carrying a toddler crawled vertically from the windows of a tipped trolley car. Surrounding it, a mob pounded the roof and undercarriage of the vehicle.

"Jesus Christ," Torres mumbled.

A loud snap on glass. Vivian spun to see a bloody handprint on the windshield. To her right, a fireman in full gear yanked a woman away by her hair. In his other hand, he held an ax.

"Help me," she screamed and reached forward. Vivian reached back, but the side window blocked her hand.

"Stay here." Torres pulled his gun.

"Wait," she said. "We have to get to the police station."

"You want me to leave her out there?" he asked.

"You can't save them all. This will spread to more people if we don't stop Mister Vincent."

He flipped on the car's floodlight, opened his car door, and used it for cover.

He aimed at the fireman. "Let her go."

On the sidewalk, an old man with blood smeared over his mouth stopped masturbating. He stared at Vivian with the same blank face that she'd seen on the priest. A teenage girl walked from behind a minivan, dragging a tire iron across the asphalt. She stared, too. Torres was going to get them killed.

"The lights," Vivian shouted across the cab. "Turn them off."

"Let the girl go," Torres shouted at the fireman, who threw the girl to the ground and raised the ax. Torres shot him. Immediately, the hostage girl grabbed the ax, stood, and slammed it into the fireman's back. She laughed and stepped on his body to pry the weapon loose.

To the left, a UPS truck blocked the intersection. Behind, other vehicles had already boxed them in. They smashed into each other trying back away from the riot.

"Turn off the lights." Vivian jumped out of the car. Smoke burned her lungs as she raced over to him. "They're like moths."

Several members of the mob rushed them. Torres fired, then again. A woman in a shredded business suit fell to the ground. Each gunshot drew more attention from the crowd. Now dozens of people stared at them. They closed in.

"We can't save them." Vivian pulled his arm. "If you want to stop this, we have to get to the station before Mister Vincent leaves."

Torres aimed and backed away slowly. Then they turned and ran down a darkened alley. Within seconds, she reached a chain link fence, lined with razor wire. The block on the other side of the fence had its power out, too. He pulled her next to a dumpster and into the stench of rotting grease. She listened. No footsteps.

"I don't think they followed us." He pointed past the gate. "The station is four blocks down on the left."

"How did he move so fast?" she asked. It didn't make sense. How many people could he have possibly gotten to in the last hour?

"That wasn't all his doing." He sounded angry. "Every major city is a ticking bomb. Once order breaks down, it explodes."

"Then we have to hurry." She took off her jacket and draped it across the barbed wire.

Torres pushed the dumpster against the fence. She used it to climb the gate. He followed behind. Quietly, they raced to the end of the alley.

Down the dark street on the other side, car fires smoldered. Every so often, shadows darted through the flickering smoke. Either people hiding, or waiting to attack.

"When we're out there," he whispered. "You shoot anyone that comes near you." He pulled a second gun from his ankle holster and gave it to her. "I don't care if it's Mother Teresa in a walker. You pop her right here." He pointed to his heart. "One shot."

"I got it."

"Do you?" His voice echoed from the alley's brick walls. "What are you going to do if you can't stop this Vincent guy?"

"I will."

"How? You don't even know what the fuck we're dealing with. He's too dangerous."

"If you even swing that thing in his direction." She aimed at him. "I'll kill you."

"You'd better wake the fuck up." Torres pointed his finger at her. "This isn't a game."

"Wake up," someone screeched.

"Whore," a man shouted from the other direction. "Whore. Whore."

Vivian held her breath. The voices quieted, leaving only the roar of flames, mingled with screams of pain in the distance.

"He's my son," she whispered. "You wouldn't understand."

"My daughter Alexis is in LA with her mother right now. After this city burns to the ground, where do you think this prick will head next?"

"Cody is not the monster," she said. "He didn't choose who his father is. It's not his fault."

"This is bigger than us now," he said quietly. "It's bigger than him."

"I can help him," she said.

"How?" he asked. "You don't even know where he is. Or if he's still alive."

"Don't say that," she said. "Mister Vincent told me he's in Cody Town still."

"How are you going to reach him?" he asked, but she had no answer. "If it doesn't work, you know what I have to do."

"No you won't."

"If something happens to us, no one will know what's going on."

"You're not going to touch him."

She hated herself for admitting it, but he was right. What if she couldn't stop Mister Vincent? If her baby was still inside his body somewhere, watching, she wouldn't let some stranger be the last person he saw on earth.

"Vivian—"

"I'm his mother." Her eyes welled up with tears. "It has to be me."

41

Vivian avoided debris as she followed Torres down the darkened sidewalk. The terror in her stomach amplified with each crunch of broken glass underfoot. What would happen when she found Mister Vincent? How could she possibly stop him, and what would happen to Cody if she failed?

Only one plan came to mind. Back in the hospital, when Mister Vincent first entered Cody's body, she'd grabbed his face and told her baby to come back to her. Vincent had flinched away from her way too hard.

I won't think twice about leaving you a turnip to care for, he'd said then.

Those words still haunted her, but the threat had also seemed like an overreaction. Even drugging him to bring him to Father Adrian hadn't struck that much of a nerve. He must've been afraid that she'd reach Cody somehow. That was the way she could get him back. She had to hold him, and talk her baby into waking up from Cody Town. It was her only option now. But how could she possibly do it without being infected by his touch?

She tripped and regained her footing. Looking down, she saw a girl, dead on the sidewalk. Somebody had taken the time to cover up her face and the top of her torso with a trench coat. Her ponytail lay unhidden. Vivian broke down in tears.

"What's going on?" Torres whispered. "Hurry up."

He stopped. Then he walked back and put his arm around her.

"I'm so sorry," she told him, but it wasn't enough.

"You didn't kill these people."

"I should have told you about Cody this morning."

"Then we'd probably both be dead now," he said. "And there'd be no one in his way."

"When we find him. If I can't stop him—"

"You will."

"I'm serious." She looked up at him. This couldn't wait. "In order to get to Cody, I have to touch his face like before. Hold him, and try to bring him back to me before he can turn me." She wiped her eyes. "Jesus, that's fucking stupid. Who knows if it will even work?"

"Listen to me Vivian." He glanced around, apparently to check for safety. Then he turned back to her and gently grabbed her shoulders. "I shouldn't have yelled at you before. I've seen what you've done to protect your son from your ex-husband and his family. Stromsky. Even this

Vincent thing. If there's anything I'd stake my own daughter's life on, it's your love for Cody."

"If I can't do this though," she said. "You have to promise—"

"I won't let you live as one of the crazy people."

"It's not just that," she told him.

"You don't have to say it."

"Cody." Her eyes teared up more. "I was wrong before. I couldn't...I wouldn't be able to, you know."

"I already knew you couldn't hurt him," he said. "That's not important right now. I trust you. This is going to work, but we have to hurry."

She nodded, but she really didn't see how to send Mister Vincent away. He seemed so untouchable.

They headed back down the road. Ahead, a big rig's engine bellowed smoke. Its oval trailer blocked both lanes of traffic. Several leaks splattered fluid on the asphalt, forming a river that flowed into the sewers. Almost every car windshield on this street had been smashed.

Where was everyone? For the last two blocks, the only signs of life had been the occasional shadow racing across their paths. A few whispered voices. Sane people, probably, who were more frightened of her than the other way around.

They turned the corner, and suddenly she knew where everyone had gone. When Torres had flipped on the police car's flood lights earlier, it had drawn them. Just a few blocks down, skyscrapers burned. Flames poured from almost every floor of the buildings. That must be where everyone had gone.

"We're here," Torres whispered and pointed to the police precinct.

The glass doors were smashed, their bent frames ripped from the hinges. She raced up the front steps and moved through the torn metal.

"Look around to see if he left anything behind." Torres squeezed through the door behind her and pulled out his cell phone. "Something to tell us where he went."

Dead police officers and civilians filled the lobby. Most of them looked as though they'd been shot. She couldn't bring herself to look at the others though, who'd clearly been beaten to death. Bloodstained walls glistened in the light of several trashcan fires. A stench nauseated her.

"We're too late," she said.

"The circuits are busy." He handed her his phone. "Keep trying. I'll see if the station's radio still works."

He moved behind the front desk and disappeared into a door on the opposite side. She tried to redial. Got a busy tone. In the adjacent room, she heard Torres rummaging around. She tried again.

"Took you long enough to get here," a child's voice taunted. She spun to find Cody standing beside a vending machine.

"I want my son back." She gripped the gun that she held at her side.

"We both know that you're not going to use that."

She couldn't even bring herself to aim it in his direction, so she set it on the front desk. It wouldn't help with what she had to do anyway.

"Cody's too young for you."

"I used to think that too, but you'd be shocked at just how many helpful folks rushed right up to me today. I've never fished with dynamite before, but I imagine it feels this good, too."

"You're sick. I won't let you—"

"And if I'm so effective on my own." He cut her off. "Then it doesn't make much sense to have you out there getting in my way, now does it?"

This was it. Maybe her only chance.

"Cody?" She searched for any signs of her baby in those eyes. But she saw only hatred. And evil. And death. "Baby, if you're in there, talk to me. Anything. Please, just talk to me."

"That's not going to work." He sounded angry. Too angry. She was on the right path.

"Cody, I love you. You're dreaming right now. All you have to do is wake up. I'm here waiting for you."

He snarled and darted toward her.

❦❦❦

Far away from Cody Town now, the dead bushes on both sides of the muddy street looked like they were covered in black oil. Even the bugs were slimy black here. Cody walked up to the huge trunk of the Dead Tree.

Above, its branches filled the whole sky. Bone pinchers had landed on them and on the ground everywhere, too. When he tiptoed past them, they didn't notice him. He touched the bark on the tree trunk, but nothing happened.

"I tried to tell you," somebody said. He turned to find Little Girl. She stepped between him and the tree. "You're dead, Cody. You belong with us now."

"Let me go," he said.

"I only let you get this far because I thought you'd finally be good and come back. Don't you know we're never going to let you leave, silly?"

All the bugs began buzzing. Above, the clouds made out of bone pinchers began glowing. One of the bugs on the ground tried to bite his shoe, so he kicked it away.

"I tried to warn you." She smiled. "Now they're going to pick their teeth with your ribcage."

"Cody, I love you," Mommy called out. Her voice rumbled the entire street. Little Girl ducked and covered her head. A crack split down the Dead Tree. Blue light showed through. Then Mommy said, "I love you. You're dreaming right now. All you have to do is wake up. I'm here waiting for you."

"Mommy." He tried to squeeze through the crack in the trunk, but it wasn't big enough. "Don't leave me here!"

⌘⌘⌘

Vivian jumped back and fell to her knees. She caught one of Cody's forearms, over his long shirt. She reached for his other hand. Shit, his fingers nicked her wrist. Had it been enough to infect her with insanity? No, he'd barely touched her. She wouldn't let it. He managed to yank himself free. Then he backed away from her, down the hallway.

"You won't take my son from me." She started toward him.

Machinery whined in the distance. Louder, its gears began to grind. Needles pricked her skin. Please no. She had to fight it. Her baby was trapped. He needed her. Pain exploded behind her eyes. She screamed and clawed at her wrists.

Sounds of clanging metal filled her head. Voices began to creep through the chaos. Where was that knife? *Don't listen. Focus.* She had to hold on. Cody was still alive. She could save him. The first time she'd spun him on the merry-go-round. Those blue eyes. She was supposed to be doing something here. Where was that knife? Cody. Blue eyes.

"What is it?" Torres ran into the lobby.

That prick cop. Rotten. Corrupt. Where was that knife?

"Come here." She quietly picked up a shard of broken glass. Maybe it could even slice into stomach muscle before she broke it off. "I need you to look at this."

"Why did you scream?" He eyed her.

"I thought I heard something." She gripped the glass. Just a few more inches, and she would castrate the fucker. "You have to see this."

"Did you find Cody?"

Yes. Cody. Where was that knife? No, she was supposed to be doing something. His blue eyes. Knife. No. Her baby was trapped. How his infant fingers wrapped around her forefinger the first time she held him in her arms. Torres put his hand on her shoulder.

"Get back," she shouted.

Metallic voices screeched in her ears. He jumped away, pulled his gun, and aimed it at her.

"Where is he?" He looked around.

"No." She couldn't speak. Blue eyes. Her baby needed her. The machinery calmed, and then stopped.

Looking up with tears in her eyes, she saw Cody standing down the hallway. Flames glowed from the shattered office windows on both sides of him. Vivian stood. There was still time to save him.

"Stay down," Torres shouted at her.

"I'm fine," she said, and then pointed at Cody. The smile left his face. "My son's right there. I know how to stop him now."

Cody bolted out a side door. She raced down the hallway, jumped over a corpse that lay slumped against the wall, and pushed her way outside. Flecks of ash snowed down in the moonlit courtyard. There wasn't enough time for him to get away. He must be hiding out here.

"Hold up." Torres opened the door. He half-aimed his gun at her. "Are you trying to get yourself killed?"

"Shhh." She listened to the eerie calm. "He's out here somewhere."

"How do I know that you're not crazy?"

"You don't," she whispered. "Now go back and call for help."

"And leave you out here alone?"

"We don't have time to argue. Think of your daughter. You're the only other person who knows what's going on here. I can get my son back. Trust me."

He stared at her for a moment. Finally, he said, "You'd better know what you're doing."

A rattling grate to her left. There. Cody had almost reached the street.

"Go warn them," she shouted at Torres.

Then she chased Cody across the street. A lighthouse loomed ahead. She followed him through the tower's front doors that looked as though they'd been kicked in. Darkness. She could barely see the first few steps of a spiral staircase that led up.

A thud to her left. Somebody moaned. Immediately, she pulled out Torres's cell phone. She held it forward with one hand. The light from the display screen barely showed the lobby. Thud. Oh, God. A thirty-something woman with dark hair sat on the stairs, her toothless smile drenched in blood.

"Tick—" she whispered. "Tick—Tick." She bashed her own face into the stairway tile and stopped moving.

Vivian carefully stepped around the woman. She raced up the spiral staircase. To the top floor. Still, no Cody. Wind whipped her hair as she moved out onto the balcony that overlooked the entire city.

Her stomach dropped. He stood on top of the railing, eight stories above the concrete steps below. A fierce wind pushed him. He ducked to hold the rail for balance. She leapt forward.

"Get back." His head jerked up. "Or I'll jump."

"Come down, please." If she could just get close enough, she could grab him. Still, the five steps between them might as well have been a mile.

"I have to give you credit," he said. "Not many can resist my touch."

"It's over," she said.

"I'm just getting started."

"I know your secret." She calmed her voice. From the crazed look in his eye, she knew any little thing might cause him to jump. "You can't turn me into one of them. Detective Torres knows about you, too. He's calling for backup now."

"I can't wait for you two to tell that story," he said. "Where do you think CPS will send me first? New York or Chicago?" She stepped forward. "Keep moving." He glanced down over the railing. "I suppose this body could survive the fall. I'm betting paraplegic."

"You'll kill my son, and then what? You'll have nothing."

"Others are waiting to take his place."

"No, they're not," she said. "You told me it took you a lifetime to create Jarod. Without Cody, you're helpless for a long time. No Carmichael children in the future. Nothing."

"This was our world first." The hateful look on his face seemed to burn through her. "We won't be held back."

"And this is how you plan to run it?" She pointed over the railing. "Look."

He turned. Flames from different skyscrapers fused together. Above, several helicopters shined spotlights down on the city. Explosions. Sirens. Gunfire rattled continuously. And Jesus, even at this height, people sounded as though they were being torn limb for limb.

"It's beautiful." He stared over the balcony. For a second, he seemed lost in it.

Vivian raced forward, grabbed his shirt, and yanked him back from the edge. She cradled him in her arms.

"I want my son back," she said. "I'll never let you have him."

He struggled to break free. With both hands he reached up and grabbed her face. Each finger felt like ice picks in her skull, but the machinery didn't come back. Not with her baby in her arms.

"Cody." She stroked his hair and kissed his forehead. "Come back to me, baby. I miss you and love you."

He grabbed her face and her wrist, but this time, she only felt the warmth of his fingers. Her baby was coming back to her. She could feel him.

"I love you, sweetie. Forever and ever. Mister Vincent can't hurt us anymore. Come back to me."

Vivian stared at him as his blue eyes opened.

"Mommy." He hugged her and began to cry. "I didn't mean to let him in."

"Oh God, sweetie." She cradled him. Her chest felt like it would cave in. It was Cody. There was no doubt. "Shhh."

"I'm sorry," he said. "I didn't mean to—"

"It's not your fault, baby." She kissed his forehead and cheeks. "I'm here now. Mommy's here. It's over."

42

Vivian held Cody's hand and exited through the side door of the stone church. Nothing could lift her mood today. Not the chirping birds on the crisp breeze, nor the laughter of children as they played on the church's lawn.

Behind her a pipe organ began playing. The choir sang over wailing family members. There was no way she could have hung around after Erika's service. Too much had happened. For now, in this moment, she just needed to get away.

At the base of the steps, Detective Torres leaned against the railing. For the last week, she'd managed to avoid him. From the look in his eye, she knew that wouldn't be an option anymore. He walked up the stairs to them.

"I'm sorry to come here today," he said. "I've been trying to get in touch with you."

"I know," she said.

"We need to talk."

"Are you a policeman?" Cody asked from behind her leg, and she realized that they had never really met.

"This is Detective Torres. He's one of the good guys." She tried to pull Cody from behind her, but he clung to her. "He's a little shy today."

"Do you have a gun to shoot bad guys?" Cody asked.

"Yes." Torres kneeled next to him. "But I don't like to use it unless I have to. I'd rather just put them in jail."

Cody's interest had waned at yes. He tried to pull his arm free.

"What?" she asked. He pointed to a fountain. Stone angels appeared to dance with each other in the center. Three other kids his age stood around it throwing coins in. "Baby, I think I'm ready to leave."

"Please." He stretched the word and bounced for effect.

"Five minutes," she said. He pulled his arm free. "That suit is brand new. Do not get it wet."

He was already across the grass before she finished. After everything he'd been through, she didn't push.

"How's he doing?" Torres asked.

"No symptoms or nightmares. Have you found Stromsky?"

"Every news station is running his police sketch."

"What are we supposed to do until you find him?" she asked.

"Have you been watching television?"

She shook her head. She had tried the first day. The twenty-four hour news circus picked and pawed at the story. San Francisco had been the target of Chinese terrorists. The Avian Flu had mutated. A few geniuses predicted an impending alien invasion. As stupid as that sounded, it was probably the closest to the truth.

"I couldn't take it," she said.

"Stromsky's on the top of our watch list. Besides, if he wanted to try anything, he would've already."

"You're probably right." She prayed that was true. "Charlotte did hire him. And she just sent Cody and me a check. To keep our mouths shut, no doubt."

"No strings attached?" he asked.

"There's no such thing." She smiled. "I tore up the check. You know, I never thanked you for clearing up those charges, and for everything else. It's been a long time since I looked to the police for help."

"Not a problem," he said, "You can repay me by taking me to lunch. We need to talk."

She knew what he wanted to discuss. Could it happen again?

Glancing over, she watched Cody lean over the rim of the fountain. With his suit coat on, he reached his whole arm into the water, fished something out, and threw it back in.

Torres chuckled, and she couldn't help but laugh, too.

"I don't have any answers for you," she finally said. God, wasn't that the truth? Did anyone? She loved Cody. She'd die for him. Maybe in the end, that's all that mattered.

"I wouldn't worry though. We know how to send Mister Vincent back. Something tells me he won't try anything in the near future."

"What if he does, though?"

"Cody could've taken control at any time. He knows that now. He just didn't know how to get back to me. Besides, next time, I'll be ready."

"Yeah," he said. "I suppose you will be. Are you two going to be okay?"

She glanced over at Cody, who'd slapped the surface of the water with his open hand. He looked back at her and smiled. She thought of the road ahead, without the threat of Jarod and his family. They were free. What did that even mean? Where would they live now? She could work again. Cody would be in kindergarten next year.

"We're going to be fine," she said.

For the first time since she could remember, she began to hope.

END OF BOOK ONE

ABOUT THE AUTHOR

Christopher Allan Poe is an author and touring musician from Los Angeles, CA. He writes paranormal fiction, with an emphasis in themes that shed light on social problems for women and children.

To learn more about upcoming releases and other exciting news, please sign up on his mailing list at:

www.ChristopherAllanPoe.com

ACKNOWLEDGMENTS

This book, and my writing career, would not exist without one person in particular. Bonnie Hearn Hill, my friend and mentor, is a shining example to all artists of the possibilities when you live for your dreams.

Thank you for all that you've done for me.

In addition, I want to thank Hazel Dixon-Cooper, Dr. Dennis Lewis, and Ryan Booth for helping me hammer out THE PORTAL. Your brilliant insight has been invaluable.

Also, special thanks to Lauri Blasch for believing in this project and for her wonderful input, Faith Caminski for her fantastic eye, and everyone at Black Opal Books.